FIVE PUBS, TWO BARS AND A NIGHTCLUB

By the Same Author

fiction
Faithless

non-fiction
Into the Badlands
Bloody Valentine

FIVE PUBS, TWO BARS AND A NIGHTCLUB

JOHN WILLIAMS

BLOOMSBURY

Author's Note

The Cardiff that appears in this book is an imaginary place that should not be confused with the actual city of the same name. Anyone who knows the city may be surprised to encounter assorted landmarks – The North Star, The Custom House, and so on – that no longer exist in Cardiff today. And being an imaginary city it goes without saying that the people who inhabit it are imaginary too.

'The North Star' first appeared in slightly different form in *Fresh Blood 2* (Do-Not Press, 1997) edited by Maxim Jakubowski and Mike Ripley. 'The Glastonbury Arms' appeared in slightly different form (and under the title 'Supposed To Be A Funeral') in *Blue Lightening* (Slow Dancer, 1998), edited by John Harvey.

Published by Bloomsbury Publishing, New York and London. Distributed to the trade by St. Martin's Press

A CIP catalogue record for this book is available from the Library of Congress

ISBN 1-58234-027-7

First published in Great Britain 1999 by Bloomsbury Publishing Plc.

First U.S. Edition 1999
10 9 8 7 6 5 4 3 2 1

Typeset by Hewer Text Ltd, Scotland
Printed in the United States of America by
R.R. Donnelley & Sons Company, Harrisonburg, Virginia

For Henry

Acknowledgements

Thanks to Abner Stein for seeing a book where I saw a short story. Thanks to Maxim Jakubowski for commissioning that first story. Thanks to John Harvey for commissioning a second story. Thanks also to Peter Ayrton and Philip John for their support and encouragement. Thanks to my editor Matthew Hamilton for his faith and perception, and to my copy-editor Sarah-Jane Forder for a job well done. Thanks, finally to Charlotte Greig for everything.

Contents

Black Caesar's

The day they were due to finish building the mosque, Kenny Ibadulla was sitting in his front room with the curtains closed, watching the rugby. Wales were playing Ireland at home. Didn't know why he bothered watching it, really. You could just open the back door and, if the wind was blowing the right way, you could hear the roar from the Arms Park.

Always put him in a bad mood too. That's why he didn't like people knowing about it, knowing he still watched it. Everyone knew he used to play; it was part of the Kenny Ibadulla legend – the best outside centre Cardiff Boys ever had, at sixteen the biggest, fastest, meanest back the coach had ever seen.

'Course then he'd gone to prison, even if he was only sixteen, and that had been the end of that. And of course he hadn't given a shit, because when he came out he was the man. And he was still the man, fifteen years on. Which was why he didn't specially want people to see him throwing things at the telly when Wales's latest pathetic excuse for a centre knocked the ball on one more time.

So he was half furious and half relieved when the phone rang just as they were coming out for the second half. He picked it up and listened for a minute, then said, 'Fucking hell, not that thieving cunt. I'll be there in five, all right.'

Then he picked up his leather jacket, XXX Large and it was

still pretty snug across his shoulders, ran his hand over the stubble on his head, checking the barber had cropped it evenly, walked through to the kitchen where Melanie was chatting to her mate Lorraine, bent to kiss Melanie on the cheek and told her he was going down the club.

Out on the street he wondered, not for the first time, if building a mosque was really worth the hassle. Seeing as there was a perfectly good one in Butetown already. But then black Muslims and regular Muslims were hardly the same thing, and what Kenny was building was Cardiff's first outpost of Louis Farrakhan's Nation of Islam.

The other worry was whether it was really all right to build your mosque on the ground floor of a nightclub. Still, the club, Black Caesar's, was the only building Kenny owned, and he'd never been able to do much with the downstairs. He'd run it as a wine bar for a bit but Kenny's clientele weren't exactly wine drinkers, and the business types who were down the docks in the daytime never used it either, so he'd given that up. Then he'd tried turning it into a shop selling sportswear and stuff. He'd had the whole Soul II Soul range in but then Soul II Soul had gone down the toilet and so had the shop. Docks boys didn't believe the gear was kosher unless they were buying it down Queen Street from some white man's store.

It had been brooding on this particular question that had led Kenny to his recent spiritual conversion. He'd been up in London, Harlesden way, doing a little bit of business, and the guys he was dealing with had taken him round the Final Call bookshop there. Nearly burst out laughing at first, sight of all these guys standing around in their black suits with the red bow ties, but when they got to talking a bit, it started to make sense. Specially all the stuff about setting up black businesses in black areas.

The way Kenny saw it, he was a community leader, yet he didn't get any credit for it. He had a business already, of course; in fact he had several, but they weren't exactly respectable. That was the way it worked – people didn't mind a black man selling draw and coke. They could just about handle a black man running a club. But a black man opens a clothes shop, and the punters fuck off up town and buy their gear there. Ignorant fuckers.

So Kenny had come back a bit inspired, like. He'd done his best to explain it all to the boys, and they'd gone along with it. Which wasn't surprising given that most of them were shit scared of him, but still, most of them knew about Minister Farrakhan already, so it wasn't too difficult, once they'd customised the approach for the local conditions.

He'd thought about changing his name, calling himself El-Haji Malik or something, but then Melanie had pointed out that he already had a Muslim name. Which was true enough, of course, and his grandad had actually been a Muslim, though his dad hadn't bothered with it, specially not after he met Kenny's mum, who was a fierce bloody Baptist and the one person Kenny was not looking forward to telling about his religious conversion.

Kenny's club, Black Caesar's, was on West Bute Street, right in the old commercial heart of the docks. On a Saturday afternoon, though, the street was almost completely dead. The only faint sign of life Kenny could see came from three of his guys – Col, Neville and Mark – sat in line along the pavement outside the club, holding cans of Carlsberg. Fuckers had been raiding the upstairs bar again.

'So where is he then?' asked Kenny.

Col jerked his thumb towards the building. 'Inside, boss. Checking the wiring, he said.'

'Fucking hell, Col, you don't want to leave that thieving cunt on his own,' said Kenny, and he headed into the club in search of Barry Myers, planning officer of the Docks Development Authority.

He found him downstairs in the back room, now the business part of the mosque, looking at the pulpit.

'Jesus, butt,' said Myers as Kenny approached, 'looks just like the one they used to have down the Swedish church.'

'Hmm,' said Kenny.

'Didn't know they had pulpits in mosques, Ken.'

'Yeah, it's called the mimbar,' said Kenny, and was pleased to see a look of surprise flash across Myers's smug face.

'Oh,' said Myers after a moment, 'the mimbar, I was wondering where you kept the booze,' and he started laughing.

Kenny didn't join in, just stood there wishing he could get away with decking the bastard. But he couldn't, he knew the form and he knew a hint when he heard one. 'Fancy a drink then, Barry?'

'Don't mind if I do, Ken, don't mind at all. Just check everything's shipshape down here first.'

So the two of them went through the motions of looking around the downstairs and Kenny had to admit his boys had done a decent job. The temple itself was all painted white and was furnished with some pews and the pulpit – mimbar – all of which, as Barry had pointed out, bore a pretty fair resemblance to the fittings in the old Swedish church. Best thing was, the back wall was even facing Mecca. It was just right, Kenny thought. Serious.

The front room still had some of the display cases left over from the clothes shop, but now they held copies of the *Final Call* and a few books on black history, plus a couple of videos of Farrakhan in action, and one of the Million Man March.

There were separate entrances outside for the mosque and the club but Kenny opened a side door and led Myers upstairs. The lights were already on around the bar, and there was the unmistakable smell of draw hanging in the air. The boys had clearly popped up to relax earlier on. Myers sniffed the air too, but didn't say anything. Kenny walked round the bar and dug out a bottle of Glenfiddich, poured a large one and handed it to Myers, then cracked open a Coke for himself.

'Missing the match then, Barry?'

'Oh yes,' said the planning officer. 'Tell you the truth, Ken, I can't stand the fucking game. When the ball's not stuck in the fucking scrum, they're kicking it into touch. Give me the ice hockey any day. You been down there, see the Devils, Ken?'

Kenny nodded. He'd been a couple of times. Nice to see Cardiff doing well at something. And a lot of young boys now were into it. But far as Kenny was concerned, you were stuck with the sport you grew up with. And suddenly he felt aggrieved that this parasite Myers was dragging him away from watching it. Time to get on with the business.

'So, Barry mate, what can I do for you?' he said, putting his drink down next to Myers and folding his arms, letting a little menace creep into the air.

But Myers didn't seem to register the threat. 'Well, Kenny,' he said, 'I've been studying the records, and this kind of change of use is highly irregular. You have to think about the whole make-up of a neighbourhood, and a church – sorry, a mosque – and a nightclub in the same building . . . Well, there's a lot of ethical issues . . .'

'How much, Barry?'

Myers looked around, then shrugged, like he figured that there were a lot of things Kenny Ibadulla was capable of, but wearing a wire wasn't one of them.

'Oh, a grand up front and a ton a week should do it.'

Kenny just looked at him. The logistics of killing him flashed through his mind. The deed itself would be no problem, whip the baseball bat out from behind the bar, strike one and it would be over. Dump the body in the foundations of one of the building sites his boys were looking after. Perfect. Proper gangster business. Then he sighed inwardly and accepted that wasn't the way things worked down here.

'Fuck the grand, Barry. I've got three hundred here in my pocket. Take it or leave it. You comes back and asks for more, I breaks your fucking legs and I'll laugh while I'm doing it.' By the end of this little speech he had his face about three inches from Barry's and that seemed to do the trick.

The weasel didn't piss himself or pass out but the smile certainly disappeared. He stepped back, hacked out a laugh and said, 'Yeah, well, Ken, like I say, it'll be a tricky one to get through the committee, but three hundred'll be all right. Long as there's no complaints.'

Kenny handed over the money and Myers downed his drink and was out of the club in seconds. Kenny headed past the dance floor and opened the door to his office, turned on the TV just in time to see Wales concede a late try to Ireland and lose a match they should have won comfortably. He switched the TV off again and headed back out to the street, the urge to deck someone growing ever stronger.

He was cheered up, though, when he saw Col halfway up a ladder carefully stencilling in the outlines of the letters prior to painting the words 'Nation of Islam' over the door.

'Nice,' said Kenny, 'gonna be nice. So we'll be ready for tomorrow, then?'

'Yeah, Ken,' said Col, not turning around from his painting, 'easy. You go on home, give the missis one. See you down the Pilot later, yeah, you can sort out my bonus.'

Kenny laughed, said, 'Pay your hospital bill more like, you don't get it done,' and headed back towards Loudoun Square wondering what else he had to get sorted for tomorrow.

Tomorrow, Sunday, was set to be the mosque's grand opening. Way Kenny saw it, things would kick off about three. Have a couple of stalls and stuff out on the street, bit of music. Open the mosque up for anyone wanted to have a look, stick a video player in there running the Farrakhan tapes. Open the club up and get the disco going around six. Make it a little community dance thing.

Kenny was so wrapped up in thinking through his plans as he cut round the side of the real mosque – as he couldn't help thinking of it – that he didn't notice the noise of movement in the bushes next to him. Then there was a sudden whoop and Kenny spun round. If he hadn't checked himself just in time he would have taken the head off seven-year-old little Mikey, who had launched himself off a tree in the direction of Kenny's broad back.

'Gotcha,' said Kenny, catching the little boy and making to throw him back into the undergrowth where a couple of his mates were watching.

'C'mon then,' he said to them. 'Aren't you lot going to help your mate?' And so seconds later Kenny was buried under a heap of junior-school banditos. He played with the little gang for another five minutes or so before chasing them back in the direction of Mikey senior's flat, and then he carried on home with a positive spring in his step. Feeling well in the mood to do as Col suggested, the second he got indoors with Melanie.

That idea flew out of his head pretty quickly when the first thing Melanie said was that he'd had a phone call. Bloke with an American accent, said he was from the Nation of Islam, and he'd be coming down tomorrow, to the opening.

'Shit,' said Kenny, and sat down heavily on the sofa. This he hadn't been expecting. Of course he'd told the people up in London what he was planning. He'd bought all the videos and books and stuff from them. And they'd spoken to head office or whatever in Chicago and got the go-ahead for a new branch. But he'd thought that would have been that. He'd told the London boys about his opening, of course, and if a couple of them had wanted to come down, well that would have been no problem. But an American? Fuck.

Kenny started to work through a mental checklist. The mosque was fine, the boys had really done a good job with it. He'd got all the literature and stuff sorted out front. Got a fine-looking sister called Stephanie to work out front too. He'd got security. In fact that had all worked out very well indeed. All the guys who worked on the door for him and stuff already had the black bouncer suits. All he'd needed to do was get a consignment of red bow ties and he'd got the uniform sorted.

Then it hit him. The one thing he didn't have was a minister. He'd been so much in charge of it all that no one had mentioned who was going to be the preacher. Maybe everyone was expecting him to do it. Well, perhaps he could do it, at that.

'Mel,' he said, 'you reckon I'd make a good minister? For the mosque, like.'

Melanie looked at him for a moment, then burst out laughing.

'What's so fucking funny?' said Kenny.

'Kenny,' she said, 'when did you last say two sentences without the word fuck in them, eh?'

Kenny shook his head, then laughed too. It was true. He'd always had a filthy mouth, and it was worse when he was nervous. And, frankly, the thought of standing up in front of all his people pretending to be some kind of minister scared the shit out of him.

What he needed was someone with a bit of front and a lot of bullshit. It didn't take long for a name to spring to mind. Mikey Thompson. He hadn't spoken to Mikey since he'd heard the little bastard had started doing a bit of freelance dealing for Billy Pinto. But what the hell, Kenny Ibadulla was a big enough man to forgive and forget; he'd give Mikey a chance to redeem himself.

He picked the phone up and called Mikey's number. Tina answered.

'Who wants him?' she asked.

'Me. Kenny.'

'Oh, sorry, Ken, he's been out all day. I'll tell him you called, like.'

'No, he fucking hasn't,' growled Kenny, 'I knows he's

there. It's fucking *Blind Date* on now, innit? Telling me Mikey's missing his *Blind Date*?'

Tina didn't say anything, just put the phone down and, a few seconds later, Mikey's voice came on the line. 'Sorry, Ken, just got in, like. Whassup?'

Kenny laid things out for Mikey. Option one, he signed on as temporary minister in Kenny's mosque. Option two, Kenny broke several of Mikey's bones, just like he should have done months ago when he found out he was freelancing for fucking Billy Pinto. Didn't take Mikey too long to choose option one. So Kenny told him to come down the Pilot around nine, they'd have a chat before the club opened.

Relieved, Kenny put the phone down and went into the kitchen where Melanie was starting to sort out the tea. He put his arms round her and was just letting them start to wander up towards her breasts when the back door blew open and in piled his three little girls and a couple of their mates.

Nine o'clock, Kenny walked up to the club, checked everything was ready for the night, and headed over to the Ship and Pilot. The boys were all there in the pool-room already. Mikey and Col were on the table, laughing and passing a spliff back and forth.

'Mikey,' said Kenny, 'you still got your suit?'

'Yeah, sure,' said Mikey. 'You want me on the door tonight, boss?' Mikey loved working the door, perfect chance to check out the talent coming in, and make his mark early. Couple of jokes as he's helping them to the cloakroom, then later in the evening, when most of the blokes are too pissed to function, Mikey leaves the door, comes into the club, and eases on in. Sweet. Once in a while it even worked out.

'Nah,' said Kenny, 'least I don't think so – check it with

Col. No, Mikey, you'll need the suit for the minister number. I'll sort you out with the bow tie and the fez, like.'

'Fucking 'ell, Ken, I thought you were joking.'

'Wish I was, Mikey, wish I was.'

'But why me, Ken? You've got a bunch of boys all into this stuff good and proper. Why can't one of them do it?'

Kenny shook his head. 'They're all fucking kids, Mikey. Need a bit of experience for this job.' Kenny paused for a moment then decided to give Mikey the full story. 'See, thing is, what I need is a bullshitter. There's some Yank coming down tomorrow, from head office, like, in Chicago, wants to see we're doing things right. I need someone can give him a bit of a show.'

'Tomorrow, Ken? You're joking.'

'Tell you what, Mikey. Best thing, we go over the mosque and I show you the stuff.'

And so it was that Mikey ended up spending his evening not hitting on the sweetest young things in Cardiff, but closeted in front of the VCR watching Minister Farrakhan in action, and frantically reading back issues of the *Final Call*.

Next day, Sunday, the festivities weren't due to start till three, but the inner circle got together at the club around one. Kenny was a bear with a sore head. Hadn't got to bed till five. Kids had woken him early, and now some fucking Yank was going to come and rain on his parade.

Still, everything seemed to be coming together pretty well. The band had just showed up, on their truck. They were just going to set up in the street outside and play. Brought their own generator and everything. Like Kenny, the boys all had their black suits and red bow ties on; looked damn serious when there was a bunch of you together. Stephanie he'd seen in the front of the mosque, looking absolutely gorgeous. The cleaners had been into the club already and it was looking pretty tidy. Col was busy blowing up balloons and tying them to everything in sight. In fact it all seemed pretty damn kosher, for want of a more appropriate word.

Then the major problem came back to him. 'Where's Mikey?' he asked.

'Christ, boss, haven't you seen him?' said Mark. 'He's inside the bloody temple pretending to be Malcolm X, like.'

And indeed he was. Kenny found Mikey standing at the mimbar waving his hands around and spouting bullshit, wearing a pair of sunglasses so dark that he didn't even notice Kenny coming in. Though, Kenny being the size he was, it didn't take too long for his shadow to register on Mikey's radar. '*Salaam aleikum*, boss,' he said, whipping his glasses off.

'*Aleikum salaam*,' said Kenny without even thinking about it. It was still a greeting you heard all the time around Butetown. 'So, you ready to go, Mikey?'

'I don't know, Ken. I thought I'd just, like, welcome everyone and then read out this introduction, like,' he said, waving one of the pamphlets Kenny had brought down.

'Yeah, fine,' said Kenny, 'just go for it,' and he headed upstairs to sort out the music for the disco later on.

By three o'clock there was already a reasonable crowd built up, practically all locals, plus a few social-worker types and a photographer who said she'd try and sell some pictures to the *Echo*.

The band got going a few minutes after, running through a few Bob Marley tunes to warm everybody up. There was a steady stream of people having a look at the mosque, even a few of the elders from the regular mosque, acting like they were just passing by accidentally. The home-made patties and samosas and fruit punch were all starting to tick over nicely and the vibe was just nice, Kenny reckoned, when the limousine drew up.

The limousine was indubitably the business. Some kind of American stretch with tinted windows. It pulled up on the edge of the crowd and double-parked neatly in the middle of the street. The passenger-side front door opened first, shortly to be followed by the two back doors and finally the driver's door. Out of each door emerged a shaven-headed character in an immaculate black suit and a red bow tie. Then, a moment later, a fifth person came out, a slighter figure with the suit and bow tie and also a fez. Evidently the boss-man.

The band kept on playing regardless, chugging through Stevie Wonder's 'Isn't She Lovely', but all other activity seemed to stop as everyone stared at the new arrivals.

Kenny nodded his head quickly to a couple of his guys and they followed in his wake as he moved through the crowd towards the out-of-towners.

'*Salaam aleikum*,' he said as he approached.

'*Aleikum salaam*,' said the guy in the fez, with a pronounced New York accent.

'So you're from, like, head office,' said Kenny.

'Kamal al-Mohammed. From Chicago, yes,' said the American, cold as anything.

'Well,' said Kenny, unaccustomedly nervous in the face of this skinny Yank, 'this is the mosque here and, as you can see, we're having a bit of an opening do, like.'

Al-Mohammed inclined his head slightly. The four other guys – bodyguards or whatever they were – didn't say a word.

Kenny wasn't sure even whether they were British or American. He waited for the guy to say something and for a few seconds they were just stood there staring at each other. Then the guy shook his head irritably and said, 'So. Show me.'

'All right, butt,' said Kenny and turned to lead the way, muttering under his breath, 'I'll fucking show you then.'

The people parted to let through what was by now quite an impressive Muslim cortège, what with Kenny and his boys and the American's crew. But before they could enter the mosque al-Mohammed stopped, surveyed the crowd and then stared at Kenny before saying, 'This is a mixed event.'

Kenny didn't know what he was on about for a moment. Thought maybe al-Mohammed meant it ought to be a men-only event. Then he realised it was racial mixing he meant.

'Yeah,' he said, 'reaching out, you knows what I mean?'

Al-Mohammed didn't look too impressed but he carried on into the front part of the mosque where Stephanie was looking beautiful behind the counter. She should cheer the old sourface up, thought Kenny, but no, not a bit of it. Al-Mohammed took one look at her crop-top and said, 'Inappropriate dress for a Muslim woman.'

Stephanie just looked at him like she was watching something really unusual on TV. Kenny stayed silent and opened the door into the mosque proper. And he wasn't sure, but he reckoned his face probably fell a mile when the first person he saw in the room, standing by the mimbar, was Mark, looking impeccable in his suit and bow tie, his hair cropped to the bone, but obviously as white as can be.

'Mr Ibadulla,' said the American after a brief, painful silence, 'have you read any of the Nation's literature?'

Kenny nodded.

'Have you read perhaps our program of belief?'

'Uh,' said Kenny, but before he could go on the American cut in.

'Well, I suggest you re-read it.'

Kenny felt like he was a kid at school again. Only difference was, none of Kenny's teachers ever dared speak like that to him, at least not after what happened when he was thirteen with that science teacher.

Back out on the street, al-Mohammed took up a position at the back of the crowd looking at the band. Behind him his comrades lined up in a row, all standing with their arms folded in front of them.

When Kenny came up alongside al-Mohammed, the American turned to him and said, 'So. When will the educational part of the proceedings start?'

Christ, thought Kenny, realising it was now up to Mikey to save the day. But he smiled and said, 'Yes, indeed, brother Waqar el-Faid will be talking in just a little while, like.'

He found Mikey in the shop giving Stephanie the full charm offensive. 'C'mon,' he said, 'you're on.'

Kenny climbed up on to the band's truck with Mikey right behind him. They stood on the side of the makeshift stage till the band finished a reggaed-up 'Wonderful Tonight', and then Kenny went to the mike.

'Ladies and gentlemen,' he said, 'and all the rest of you lot. *Salaam aleikum*, and welcome to the opening of Cardiff's first Nation of Islam mosque. I'd also like to welcome our special guest, Mr al-Mohammed from Chicago. And now we're going to have a few words about the Nation of Islam from a man you all knows.' Kenny ground to a halt, wondering whether he could get away with introducing Mikey as Waqar el-Faid. He decided against it and just waved his arm in Mikey's direction before jumping off the front of the stage.

Immediately there was a muttering from certain sections of the crowd. No one had quite seen Mikey as a spiritual teacher before. The real trouble, though, it quickly became clear, was that neither had Mikey.

Mikey's speech was basically just a matter of reading out the pamphlet he'd found, but with every sentence it was falling flatter and flatter. Mikey Thompson delivering a lecture on living a clean life and running your own business was just too ridiculous. They might have taken it from an American, but from Mikey? Then he said something about the importance of respecting your women, and a voice shouted, 'You should bloody know, Mikey,' and suddenly the whole crowd was creased with laughter. Mikey just dried up. For a moment Kenny thought he might be about to burst into tears. But then Mikey started talking again.

'Listen,' he said, 'like all of you, I'm new to this Muslim bit. But you shouldn't laugh at it just 'cause it's me talking.' He paused for another couple of seconds and started again. 'I've been thinking about my little boy, little Mikey. He's seven, right, just started junior school. And I was thinking about when I was at junior school, just down the road here, same place as most of you. And I was thinking about how I didn't know I was black then.'

A woman laughed.

Mikey put his hand up. 'No, I'm not saying I was blind, love, but I didn't know what it meant to be black. Down here, down the docks, it seemed like we were all together, right. Then, when I was eleven, I went to secondary over Fitzalan, and I found out what it meant. Nah mean?'

A rumble of agreement came from the crowd.

'What I found out, right, was that the rest of the people out there think they knows what you are if you come from Butetown. Right. So what I'm saying, and I'm going to shut up now, so don't worry, is that if we're going to make something of our lives, we've got to do it ourselves. And that's why I say that, whatever you think about Kenny here – and I know a lot of you may have had your troubles with Kenny – you've got to respect what he's doing.' And with that he too jumped off the stage.

The applause Mikey got wasn't exactly wild, but still, when he came down into the crowd, several people clapped him on the back and said well done. One or two of the sisters gave him 'Mikey, I never knew you were so sensitive'-type looks, which he returned with his most sensitive wink. Kenny walked over and clapped him on the back too, then turned round to see what his guests had made of it.

He found them standing in formation once more, this time outside the entrance to the club.

'What's this, brother Ibadulla?' asked al-Mohammed, pointing at the sign saying 'Black Caesar's Dancing and Dining'.

'It's a club,' said Kenny.

Al-Mohammed looked at his coterie and then looked back at Kenny. 'You're going to place Allah's temple underneath a nightclub, brother Ibadulla?'

'Well, there are separate entrances,' said Kenny, sounding feeble even to himself.

Al-Mohammed shook his head. 'Show us inside,' he said.

Kenny looked at his watch. Half five. The club was due to open in thirty minutes. That would probably be the last straw for these guys. He had to get them in and out and fast, before people started banging on the doors. So he sighed, opened the door and led the way upstairs into the club. Lloyd the barman was busy washing glasses but otherwise the place was deserted. Al-Mohammed just looked at the bar, shook his head once more and uttered the one word 'alcohol' before saying, 'Mr Ibadulla, let's go into your office. We have much to discuss.'

Kenny shrugged, thinking to himself, this is the thanks you get for trying to put something back into the community. He unlocked the office door, ushering the visitors inside.

The last man in shut the door behind him, and in an instant Kenny found himself looking straight down the barrel of a gun.

Al-Mohammed was the man holding the gun, and once Kenny had registered its presence he started talking again, only this time his voice had no trace of a New York accent. Instead it was pure Brummie.

'All right, Kenny mate. Had you going there, eh!'

Kenny shook his head in absolute and total disbelief. He'd let the Handsworth crew jerk him about like a prize bloody twat.

The Handsworth crew were evidently of the same mind. Two of the bodyguards were shaking with suppressed laughter. 'Inappropriate dress for a Muslim woman,' said one of them. The other grinned and rolled his eyes and, for a moment, Kenny thought he might have an opening.

The leader, however, kept his gun firmly trained on Kenny and said, 'Now, Mr Ibadulla, how about you open your safe and we have a look, see if there's anything we like in there.'

Kenny was a pro. He didn't do anything stupid. Just swore under his breath at his gullibility and tried to remember just how much he was holding in the safe. Around seven and a bit, he figured, and sighed as he opened up.

The former al-Mohammed kept his gun steadily on Kenny as his cohorts loaded the contents into a couple of black canvas bags. One of them then stepped behind Kenny, who wondered for a moment whether he was about to die, before a voice said, '*Salaam aleikum*, mate', and unconsciousness hit him like a freight train.

When Kenny came to, ten minutes later, after being given a good shaking by Col and Mikey, he discovered what had happened next. The Brummies had held a gun on Lloyd behind the bar, then knocked him out too. Then they'd walked downstairs and out of the club, back in character, shaking their heads and acting disgusted by what they'd found. The crowd had parted to let them make their way to the limo. A couple of the youth had catcalled them as they drove away, but that was that. The band had launched into Seal's 'Crazy' and it had taken a few minutes for anyone to wonder why Kenny hadn't come back down.

'Shit,' said Mikey, when Kenny told him what had happened. 'Don't know about you, Ken, but I don't think we're cut out for the religious life.'

The North Star

The baby, Jamal, woke up at eight. Maria rolled over once, buried her head in the pillow and tried to ignore him but it was no good, so she fetched him from his cot and brought him into the bed with her. There was plenty of room. Bobby must have left some time in the middle of the night. Though when they'd got to bed it had been late enough already, couldn't have been before four.

Anyway, Jamal went back to sleep for an hour, so she did too, and by then it was nine o'clock and Donna was up and played with him for a couple of hours so she managed to kip on and off till eleven, which was a result. It had been a hard night.

Maria got up, dug out a fresh pair of black jeans and a pink blouse, then rifled through last night's pockets to see how much money she had left. Forty quid. She was sure she'd taken at least a hundred yesterday. Where had it gone?

Looking at her face in the bathroom mirror, even after a good long shower, she could still trace where most of it had gone. Her eyes were bloodshot from the booze, her pupils dilated from the coke – or at least what Bobby swore blind was coke, tasted more like weak sulphate – her whole face puffy from the tranks she'd taken to get to sleep. Fifty quids' worth of hangover, any way you looked at it.

Still, she was only twenty-two, she could handle it. And she was a mother too and she could handle that, not like some people she knew.

Jamal was sitting in his highchair with a yoghurt pot in front of him and most of its contents around his mouth. Donna was watching *Richard and Judy*. Maria kissed Jamal and ruffled his black hair and made a cup of tea. Drank that with four paracetamols and she felt halfway human. Sitting on the sofa with Jamal on her knee watching a cooking show, she could feel a memory nagging at her. Something from last night. It wasn't something she'd done, there was none of that guilt or embarrassment lurking there; it was something good, but what?

Getting Jamal ready to go out, zipping him into his miniature puffa, she remembered. It was one of the ship boys, a German boy in from Rotterdam, in the club last night. A little bit of smuggling business he needed a hand with. Her and Bobby had looked at each other, lightbulbs popping up in bubbles on top of their heads. Both thinking the same thing, you better believe it.

Walking down Bute Street with Jamal in his pushchair, she tried to recall the details but they obstinately refused to come. So halfway down she stopped at the phone and called Bobby. Bobby sounded half asleep, but brightened when Maria mentioned the ship guy, and suggested they meet up at the Hayes Café in a couple of hours, when Maria had done her shopping.

So Maria carried on walking, happy to be out and about on a fine sunny May day. Stopped every couple of minutes for her mates to admire Jamal. Even the old biddies who wouldn't talk to her would stop and have a look at Jamal, who was so sweet with his blue eyes and golden-brown face, and they could see she looked after him well.

She wondered if his eyes would stay blue. He was eighteen months now, so she supposed they probably would. Weird, but nice; showed there was a lot of her there.

Passing the Custom House, she saw John the landlord bringing in a couple of crates of Hooch. He waved and dashed inside, came out with a lollipop for Jamal.

'Col must be proud of him, eh?'

Col was her baby's father. And he was a nice bloke, as it went, though full of all this Twelve Tribes bollocks. His main contribution to Jamal's upbringing was to come round and make sure she wasn't feeding him any pork. Not that he'd been coming round much at all lately; he couldn't really handle her scene with Bobby.

'Yeah. He thinks you're pretty safe, don't he,' she said, tickling Jamal under his chin.

'Yeah, well, give him my regards, tell him to stop by if you see him.'

Oh right, she thought, running a little low on the ganja, are we? Still, you had to hand it to Col. He'd been going on about all this back-to-the-land shit for years and now he was doing a tidy little business with this hydroponic gear.

She carried on under the bridge, past the Golden Cross, exchanged 'hiya love's with one of Col's aunties and thought about going into Toys'R'Us for a moment. Then she pictured the mountain of toys Jamal already had that he couldn't play with yet. Still, what was the use of having some money if you couldn't spend it on your kid? So she carried on to Mothercare, bought him a couple of new outfits, went into the St David's Centre and mucked about in Boots for a while, buying some nice stuff for herself. Just had a few minutes to get a carton of cheap fags and a bit of food from the market, and it was time to meet Bobby.

The Hayes Island Snack Bar looked like an old park caff that had been accidentally dropped slap bang in the city centre. Bobby was sitting at one of the tables over near the public toilets, a cup of coffee in front of her, brazenly staring down the passers-by.

'All right, girl,' said Bobby, and Maria's heart leapt. She could swear it really did jump inside her as she looked at Bobby, this stocky black girl with the short locks who was the strongest person she'd ever met. Sat there in a black Adidas tracksuit looking for all the world like a fourteen-year-old boy, though she must be thirty at least. Maria just wanted to throw herself at her. She wanted to eat her.

Bobby was her pimp.

Bobby insisted on that. 'I'm a pimp, me,' she'd say, flashing her gold tooth. 'Top pimp.'

Maria gave Bobby money.

But it wasn't like Bobby had some stable of bitches, like they say in the down-in-the-hood movies. Bobby was Maria's girl. It's just that that's how it is when you hustle. Someone who shares their life with a hustler, they're a pimp. Maria buys a can of baked beans and gives half to Bobby. Immoral earnings. Hey, one day, Maria thought, she'd like to see someone who had some moral earnings. Colliers. Yeah, right. At least with what she did you knew you were getting fucked.

And Bobby had respect. All the lesbians – Christ, she didn't like that word – the lesbian pimps on the scene had respect. The men, though, that was another story. They couldn't handle it. Couldn't handle their woman hustling. Sure, they'd take the money all right, but then they'd disrespect you. It pissed her off. She knew she was fit, she knew how men looked at her before they knew, and she saw how they looked at her after. Weaklings. Not like Bobby.

Bobby picked Jamal out of his pushchair. Bobby loved Jamal, was always criticising the way Maria dealt with him. Half the time, people who didn't know saw them together, they'd swear Bobby was Jamal's big brother. Same colouring. Bobby never talked about her mam and dad; she'd talked about a home, though. Surprise.

'You remember the guy, then, last night,' Maria said once she'd got herself a tuna sandwich and a piece of toast for Jamal.

'Yeah,' said Bobby, 'so you going to do it or what?'

The ship guy had told Maria, back in the North Star, luxuriating in the aftermath of the blowjob she'd given him in the car-park, that he had a k of the good stuff, prime coke, on the boat. But he was hinky about bringing it on shore and double hinky about who to sell it to. He was young – no more than nineteen, she figured – and she could see that this was a boy jumping out of his depth and hoping he could swim. Mind the sharks, boy, she felt like saying, but naturally didn't. Instead she listened to his worries about getting past the checkpoints on and off the boat, and told him it was no problem, bring a girl on and they'll turn a blind eye.

Really, he'd said. Yeah, really, she'd said, been doing it long enough.

'But who am I going to deal with?' he'd asked. 'I don't know this town.' Like he knew anywhere.

'Relax,' she'd said, 'I'll bring the gear out for you, and sort you out with a deal, you just cut me a little taste,' and she'd squeezed his dick and half an hour later she'd done him again in the back of a car. When the North Star closed he was almost begging her to meet him again.

'All right,' she'd said, 'see you here, midnight tomorrow. We'll sort your little problem out.'

'Yeah,' she said to Bobby, 'he'll be easy.'

Bobby laughed and contorted her face into a parody of sexual ecstasy. Jamal saw her and laughed too, shouting Bobby's name and clapping his hands together.

Coffee finished, Bobby wanted to buy some new trainers, so they trekked round Queen Street checking out the options before Bobby went for a pair of Adidas, white stripes on black to match her tracksuit, in a boy's size. By then Jamal was hungry again so they dined at the sign of the Golden Arches and then headed back towards Butetown, making plans for the night ahead.

Bobby peeled off at the Custom House to play pool with the other pimps and the girls on the afternoon shift. Maria kind of missed the afternoon shift. For a start, you were less vulnerable in daylight and for seconds you really felt like you were putting one over on the poor stiffs sweating in McDonald's, spending your afternoons drinking and shooting pool and smoking with just the odd couple of minutes behind Aspro Travel Agents to earn your wedge.

Still, it worked pretty well for her now too. She could spend all day with Jamal and just go out to work once she'd put him to bed. Donna was always there to babysit. Donna was the only girl she knew that used to pretend to be a hustler, 'cause it made it sound like she had a sex life. It wasn't that she was ugly, really – well she was, but that never had much to do with anything, you should see some of the girls out there on the beat and they did all right. It was just she was such an ignorant mouthy cunt. Still, she was good to Jamal.

Eight o'clock, Jamal was asleep and Maria spent the last of her money on a cab down to the Custom House. Bobby wasn't there, must have gone back home for her tea, so Maria cadged her first can of Breaker off Paula, a big girl from up the valleys somewhere who was already starting to show. 'Only three months,' she said, pissed off.

Half an hour later there was still no sign of Bobby, so Maria thought fuck it and went out on the beat, shared a spliff with a couple of girls and was just getting fed up with waiting around when a carload of Asians showed up. Normally she wasn't too keen on bulk deals but she'd never had any trouble with Asians. Bloody mainstay of the trade, they were; poor geezers over from God knows where to work in some cousin's restaurant for fifty quid a week. No chance of an arranged marriage till they got their own balti house, hardly surprising they came down here for a quick one.

So she bent down to the window and bargained a bit. Made a deal. For eighty quid she'd take the four of them back to the flat and do them all.

She was just doing number two when Bobby burst in, blue in the face, saying she needed a word. Poor bloke inside her didn't know where to put himself, so she told Bobby to fucking behave and wait outside, got number two back in the saddle and off in two minutes flat, which wasn't bad going as it goes. Then she went out to the living-room and found numbers one, three and four looking fed up while Bobby gave Donna a hard time about something or other. Not keeping Jamal's toys tidy enough, probably.

'Now,' said Bobby, 'I've got to talk to you *now*.' So Maria had a quick word with Donna, got her to do number three for a twenty-quid rake-off. Sent numbers one, two and four out to the chip shop, and once all the doors had closed asked Bobby what the fuck she was playing at.

'No,' said Bobby, crowding her into a corner like she was a tough guy, which was comical, really, as Maria was a good three inches taller than her, but, still, she let Bobby have her fun. 'It's what you've been playing at. Who you've been talking to.'

'What?'

'Kenny Ibadulla knows about tonight.'

'Shit.'

'So how comes, eh? How comes Kenny knows my business, you stupid slag?'

'I'm sorry, Bob,' said Maria, realising what had happened and compensating by letting the tears start. She was always a great crier, Maria.

Bobby was a pushover. She stepped back, said, 'All right, love, who did you tell?'

'Terry. Fucking Terry. Except I never told him, he was just sitting next to me and Hansi.'

'Hansi?'

'The sailor, right, and Terry was there, but I thought he was too out of it to notice what was going on, and anyway I didn't think he was talking to Kenny.'

'Yeah, well, maybe this is Terry's way of getting back in the good books.'

Then the bell rang and Maria let in the three punters who sat down and politely offered their chips around. Number three was still in with Donna – must have been a good eight minutes, which outraged Maria's professional soul – so she ate one more chip and took number four into her room and had him back out again just as number three came out of Donna's.

'Any time, boys,' she said as she closed the door on the blokes. Bunged twenty to Donna and then sat down with Bobby to figure out what the hell to do about Kenny Ibadulla.

Quarter to twelve, they went over to the North Star. No sign of Terry or Kenny, though it was unlikely Kenny would show in person. Kenny was a gangster, all right, but these days he thought he was too good to hang around with hustlers.

Around ten past twelve, Bobby was just lighting up a spliff and Maria was dancing with one of the Barry girls to an old Chaka Khan record when Hansi the sailor came in. He was about five nine, dark-haired with a rather sorry-looking tache. He was with three other blokes from the ship, looked like they were probably German as well.

They stood in the centre of the room for a moment, eyes adjusting to the gloom, checking the place out. Hansi saw Maria on the dance floor and waved. Then one of his mates, a six-foot redhead, went over to Maria and the Barry girl and asked them if they wanted a drink. They both said yeah and soon they were all sat around a table drinking cans of Pils. The North Star didn't run to draught beer, which was probably just as well, the amount Stevo behind the bar bothered with keeping the place clean.

Bobby sat at the bar, smoking her spliff, watching them. After a while she went over to another couple of girls, Sue from Merthyr and Big Lesley, and told them the sailors were loaded and in the mood to go back to the ship for a party.

Around one, everyone seemed to be having a good time and the German boys were definitely in the mood for action.

So Maria led the way out of the club and, linking arms with Hansi, headed for the hulk of the *Queen of Liberia.*

Out in the open, it was obvious that Hansi was nervous as shit but, when Maria pulled him closer and whispered in his ear what she was going to do to him when they got to the ship, he brightened up.

As predicted, there was no problem with security when they got to the ship. The watchman was out for the count, a telltale can of Tennent's Super on his desk. On board ship, they piled into an empty mess-room, started passing around a bottle of vodka one of the Germans produced and some spliff that Big Lesley had rolled up. Maria began to notice that Hansi wasn't really all that friendly with the other guys. 'Ozzie,' they called him, and from the way he reacted she could tell it was a nickname and not a friendly one.

So, after twenty minutes or so, she said, 'Let's go back to your cabin,' and it was with obvious relief that Hansi agreed.

'Some problem with your mates?' she asked, worried that they might have wind of Hansi's deal.

'No,' he said, 'they just don't like me because I'm from the East.'

'Oh right,' she said, and started rubbing the front of his jeans to get his mind back on track.

In his cabin she started taking his jeans off while detailing what she was going to do for him. Experience had told her that talking up her act in advance was just as effective and a lot easier than actually running through her bag of tricks. And so it proved with Hansi. By the time she had him in her mouth, he was primed and ready. Thirty seconds later she was rinsing her mouth out in the basin and he was sitting back on his bunk looking a little crestfallen.

'Five minutes,' he said, 'five minutes and we go again, yes?'

At his age, she thought, he probably wasn't joking. It was time to get things moving on. 'Plenty of time later for that,' she said, giving his hair a quick ruffle, 'but if we're going to get out of here while your mates are still busy, we'd better be going.' He nodded and stood up. She hoped to hell he was understanding everything she said.

'You wait outside,' he said, and he shooed her out of the cabin. A minute later he came out too, a little black canvas bag over his shoulder.

'Let's go,' he said, and they headed back off the ship. This time there were a couple of official types standing by the watchman's office. They looked dubiously at Maria and Hansi for a moment and said something in German to Hansi, but Maria started licking Hansi's ear and he did a creditable impersonation of a drunken sailor walking his girl back to shore, and after a brief hard stare one of the officer types waved them by.

Back in the North Star, Bobby was waiting for them. As Maria and Hansi came in, she ushered them to a table at the back where the darkness was almost total. 'Is that it?' she said, prodding the bag Hansi held clasped between his knees.

He nodded and she hefted it, testing it for weight, though Hansi never let go of the bag. Then he proffered it to Bobby and she dipped a finger in and took a taste from the top, which was all she could get at. Tasted good to her.

'Yeah, that'll do,' she said. 'Now, how much d'you want for it?'

'Fifty thousand marks,' he said, puffing himself up a little but his eyes giving him away, nervously looking around the room, realising how little control he had over the situation.

'Yeah, what's that in pounds?'

Neither Bobby nor Maria had much of a clue about exchange rates, but they knew what a k of Charlie went for and, when Hansi came back with, 'Twenty thousand,' after thinking for a moment Bobby almost found herself nodding.

'Fuck off,' she said. 'Five grand, tops.'

'OK,' said Hansi, smiling now.

'Half an hour,' said Bobby. 'You stay here with Maria, I'll be back with the money.'

Forty minutes later, Bobby was back, ten grand in her jacket after a rendezvous with Billy Pinto, who she knew was looking for a decent score, let him take a bit of Kenny's market. Billy had jumped at the deal. Turn the k into rocks, and he'd be doing some serious business. And 'cause he lived over Ely, with a bit of luck Kenny would never figure out who sold him the gear.

'Hansi,' she said, 'fucker beat me down to four grand.' And she started discreetly counting out the money.

Hansi suddenly looked harder and older than before. A lock-knife appeared below table height, jabbing into Maria's leg.

'You want me to cut your girlfriend here? By this artery?' he said. 'Or you want to pay me my money?'

'Christ,' said Bobby, 'calm down, mate. Only trying it on.' And she kept on counting till she got to four grand, then dipped her hand into her pocket and pulled out another wedge. 'Here's your five grand, like I said.'

Hansi had the money inside his leather jacket before Bobby had time to blink. He stood up, the knife still held inside his sleeve, bowed slightly to Maria and a moment later he was gone.

'Shit,' said Maria.

'Don't worry, girl,' said Bobby, and leaned closer to her and told her how much money they'd cleared.

Maria said nothing for a moment, just thought about the changes five grand could make to her life. 'C'mon,' she said, 'let's get back to the flat.'

They were almost at the flat door when they heard the footsteps behind them, coming up the stairs. Maria had the door open and Bobby was half through it when, for the second time in ten minutes, Maria felt a knife pressing against her flesh. It was Billy Pinto holding the knife and neither he nor his two associates looked too well pleased with life.

Bobby and Maria were bundled into the flat. Billy made them sit next to each other on the couch and then got right down in Bobby's face. 'What the fuck,' he said, 'what the fuck d'you think you're doing, trying to rip me off like that?'

'What?' said Bobby.

'That kilo of crap you sold me. Coke on the top; fuck knows what underneath. I wants my money back, girl.'

'Shit,' said Bobby, looking at Maria.

Maria shook her head in genuine disbelief. She really couldn't credit that Hansi had had it in him to pull off a stunt like this. No wonder he'd looked nervous.

'So where's my money?' said Billy.

'Bill,' said Bobby, 'it's not our deal. It's this sailor. He's the one who's ripped you off.'

'I don't think so, Bob,' said Billy, 'I don't think it was no sailor came round my house, told me she had a kilo of gear. It wasn't no sailor took my ten grand.' He paused for a moment and stared at Bobby. 'And I'll bet it wasn't no sailor got the ten grand either. How much you holding, Bob?'

Bobby considered holding out for about a millisecond. Then she sighed and said, 'I've got five, Billy, take that and we'll get you the other five back. Just let go of us, right.'

Billy walked over, took the five grand from Bobby's pocket. 'Yeah, you'll pay it back, all right, but first you're going to have to learn a lesson.'

'Not here,' said Maria, the first thing she'd said since things went to hell. 'My boy's sleeping. Not here.'

Billy nodded. 'All right, I knows just the place.'

Billy led the way down the stairs, Bobby and Maria following, Billy's guys right behind them.

Halfway down the second flight, Maria suddenly clutched her stomach and collapsed to the ground. 'Fuck,' she said, 'the baby.'

It worked a treat. Billy and his guys stopped as one, looks of horror on their faces. Bobby whipped the legs from under the guy nearest to her, sent him tumbling down the stairs. A second later she had her own knife out and started swinging it in an arc in front of her, keeping Billy and the other guy away. Meanwhile Maria was back on her feet and kicking the guy who'd fallen downstairs hard in the face before he could get back up. And then the two women were off, flying down the remaining stairs into the lobby.

And smack into the ample frame of Kenny Ibadulla. There was Kenny and Terry and another bloke standing there, Kenny with a gun in his hand. Billy and his boys arrived on the scene a second or two later and Kenny shifted around so the gun was pointed squarely at Billy. And then everyone started talking at once. Five minutes later everyone had some idea what the situation was, and it was clear that it was up to Kenny, as the man with the gun, to dictate what happened next.

'Billy,' he said, 'you fuck off out of this. You want to be some big-time dealer, boy, you stay up in fucking Ely and do it there. Now fuck off. You'll get your money.'

And, at that, Billy and his boys slunk off, doing their best to look like it was their own decision.

Then Kenny turned to Bobby and Maria. 'Now, Bob,' he said, 'I got to pay Billy five grand. And you know what that means?'

Bobby nodded.

'Right, that means you owe me five grand. And how are you going to get that for me? Your girlfriend going to make it for me? Lying on her back? Or you got some better idea?'

'The ship guy,' Bobby said.

'Right,' said Kenny, 'the ship guy. He's the one to blame, inne? But he's not my problem.' By now Kenny was virtually standing on top of Bobby, letting his size and weight work for him. Then he turned and pulled back. 'You've got till daylight. You haven't got my five grand back by then, you'll be working for me.'

And so Kenny and his boys left, and Maria and Bobby sat together on the stairs for a moment, holding each other and shaking. Maria thought she was going to hyperventilate. The prospect of owing Kenny Ibadulla didn't bear thinking about. Christ knows what the interest payment on five grand would be – a hundred a week, at least. Working for herself and Bobby and Jamal was one thing: working for that arrogant bastard was something else entirely, specially as he most likely wouldn't pay Billy the money anyway.

'Shit. Shit. Shit,' she said. Then she had an idea.

'C'mon,' she said to Bobby. 'We've got to get back to the North Star.'

It was four o'clock, closing time in the North Star; but luck was with Maria when a couple of sailors came out with Lorna, one of the Barry girls. It was no trouble for Maria to join the party, and ten minutes later she was back on board the ship. Five minutes of wrestling in another mess-room with a drunken sailor, and she was able to beg off to find a toilet. Ten more minutes of floundering around the ship and she found Hansi's cabin. Took a deep breath and knocked.

He looked horrified at first, but Maria pretended not to notice and stuck to her script like the trouper she was. 'Hansi, baby, I've come back to celebrate, I would have come straight back with you but I had to dump that dyke Bobby.' And before his brain could start functioning, she carried straight on into, 'Hansi, I need you inside me,' and started pulling his clothes off.

And it worked. He let her. He let himself believe that he was such a slick piece of work that he could screw the girl over the deal and still screw her all night long with no come-back. Just sail away in the morning.

She had to do it twice, but the second time she got her result. He fell asleep. It didn't take long to search the cabin. First thing she found was a washbag that weighed far too much. Inside it was another kilo of white stuff. God alone knew whether this one was real or fake, but she scooped it up anyway and a moment later she found the five grand stuffed in a sock.

Five minutes later, she was starting to panic. The boat was a total bloody maze. Once she'd found herself in the rec room they'd all been in earlier, but she must have taken the wrong exit, 'cause where the hell she was now she had no idea, except the cabins were looking a bit posher.

She could have sworn she must have walked down the same corridor three times, when what she was dreading finally happened. A door opened and she walked slap bang into one of the handsomest men she'd ever seen in her life. She had him pinned instantly as a type, the Latin lover. Fair enough in private life, but a pain in the arse in her professional life. They'd spend hours trying to get you to look like you were doing it for fun not fifty quid. Anyway, last thing she needed right now, Casanova in his boxers.

'Uh,' she said, 'I was looking for . . .'

'Yes?' he said, his eyes giving her the old up and down. 'You were looking for something?' There was a pause. 'A man maybe?'

Jesus, thought Maria, here we go, and started to shake her head.

' 'Cause you come to the wrong place here, darling,' he said, and Maria actually did sigh with relief.

'No,' she said, 'I was just looking for the way out.'

'No problem, sweetie,' said the bloke, and popped back into his room for a dressing-gown. Maria followed, dumb with gratitude, as the guy swished his way up a flight of stairs, along a couple of corridors and out to the gangway. The face of the guard on duty was a picture when he saw who it was, waving Maria goodbye off the ship.

Bobby was waiting for her in the car-park and Maria just collapsed in her arms. Bobby wrinkled her nose for a moment at the smell of her, but never let go.

Six thirty a.m., Bobby knocked on Kenny's door. Woke his wife up, who shouted at her to get her perverted black arse out of there, but then Kenny came to the door and let her in. She handed him the coke, Kenny tasted it, from the top, the bottom and the middle, nodded and told Bobby she was cool.

'And what about Billy?' said Bobby.

Kenny laughed, said, 'Billy's my problem. Be cool.'

Coke talking, thought Bobby. Everyone's a superman with coke. And walked back up to Maria's place.

Maria's already celebrating, got a bottle of champagne from round Bab's. Opens it as Bobby comes in the door, stuff sprays everywhere, must have been warm as fuck. Jamal's jumping up and down with excitement.

'Tell you what,' says Bobby, 'why don't we go for a little holiday? Just the three of us, like.'

'Yeah,' says Maria, 'you serious?', her eyes going wide, like it's the biggest treat anyone's ever offered her, like it wasn't her got the five grand that's sitting on the table.

'Yeah,' says Bobby, 'let's just get a cab out the airport. We'll get the first plane going somewhere hot.' And Maria jumped up and threw her arms round Bobby, hugging her hard. Jamal did the same to her knees, and for a moment Bobby felt like it was more than her heart could stand. A couple of minutes later, she picked up the money and carefully put it into the inside pocket of her jacket.

Six o'clock that evening, Bobby, Maria and Jamal were in Tenerife.

Two weeks later they came back.

Week after that, Maria was back outside the Custom House and Bobby was playing pool inside. You know what they say – you have to hustle in this life.

The Four Ways

Mikey felt it was time he got in on the pimping game. Doing the shops had done him fine over the years, apart from the once, but there came a time when you knew you were pushing your luck. He'd tried dealing. He wasn't exactly giving up on that either – if you wanted to buy something, little bit of weed, a couple of Es, well he could sort you out, no trouble at all – but moving up in that world was a problem. Some well heavy geezers in that world. For instance, the thing that happened with Deandra's cousin, down from Birmingham there. Mikey had told him he had a line on some serious Charlie, fresh off the boat. It had just been the brew talking, but a week later the guy's back down in Cardiff saying, 'Mikey, I'm in the market – now set me up.'

So Mikey had acted like he was the man and called Kenny, who'd told him to fuck off, no way he was dealing with no Brummies. So then he'd called Billy Pinto over in Ely there, and Billy had only come to the meet with a fucking shotgun, and the guy from Edgbaston or Handsworth, or whatever balti-house place he came from, had freaked out and opened up with some joker pistol, looked like his grandad had brought it back from World War Two, and Mikey had done the only sensible thing and legged it, and now the Pintoes were out for his blood for setting them up with some Brummie psycho, and the Brummie psycho was threatening all kinds of shit, and frankly drugs were fine but Mikey was looking for something a little less dangerous.

So, Wednesday morning, Mikey decided to get up early. First step was to get out of the house without any bother from Tina. Best way to do that, he'd found, was to say he'd take little Mikey to school. That way Tina didn't get her fat arse out of bed and, once Mikey was out of the house, that was the hard part done. So he was up at eight thirty. Little Mikey was already sitting in the living-room with a bowl of cereal next to him. *The Big Breakfast* was on the TV, but little Mikey wasn't watching it; instead he was bent over a picture he was drawing – Spiderman fighting some villain or other. Spidey was swinging up the side of a building, little Mikey concentrating hard on getting the web right.

Mikey had a quick hit of Lucozade Sport from the fridge, checked his hair carefully in the mirror and wondered, as he often had the last few months, whether he should go for a total skinhead like a lot of the boys these days. But he knew that looking hard was tricky when you were five foot four so, splashing on a spot of aftershave, he decided to stick with the flat-top do, gave him an extra inch or so on top.

Quarter to nine, he had little Mikey out of the house, wearing his coat even in May because Tina was terrified about his asthma. It was only five minutes down to the school, but Mikey made a habit of getting there a little early. Lot of fit women taking their kids into school. And taking your own seven-year-old in was perfect camouflage, showed you were a nice guy. Wolf in sheep's clothing – that's the way Mikey liked to think about himself. Being small helped too, he thought, meant they didn't take him seriously till it was too late.

So, as they got to the playground, he shooed little Mikey

in, to play football with the boys, and stood around chatting with Tina's mate Lesley and her friend Ruth-Ann, who was wearing some kind of Lycra sports top that had Mikey's attention pretty well occupied at eye level. Ruth-Ann was out of the question, though; he knew who she was seeing and no way was he going sniffing round that yard. So, after a moment or two, he let his eyes wander away from Ruth-Ann's chest and let them alight on a girl named Tyra.

Tyra, he thought, might be a prospect. So he made a couple of lewd suggestions to Lesley and Ruth-Ann, laughed as they made to batter him, and waved goodbye. Then timed things nicely so he brushed up against Tyra as they squeezed out of the school gate.

'Whassup, girl?'

'Nothing,' said Tyra, who was long, tall and light-skinned. She'd been in school with Mikey, a couple of years younger, ran with Mikey's sister Lisa for a bit, but she never gave him the time of day. Never had since either, never went for his bullshit at all, never laughed at it like you were supposed to. Fucking stuck-up piece, in fact, if you asked Mikey, but she'd come down with a bump lately, what he'd heard. Two kids in school, and now her man inside, little matter of armed robbery over a bookie's in Canton. What Mikey'd heard was Tyra had been seen out hustling. She had to be a prospect, just a matter of getting the pitch right.

'Sorry to hear 'bout Tony.'

'Long fucking time you waited to tell me that.'

'Yeah, well I was thinking, maybe you could do with a few new clothes, for the kids, like.'

Tyra kept walking but betrayed her interest by not saying anything. You see, Mikey's talent was pretty well known – it was generally agreed around Butetown that no one could shoplift like Mikey. You wanted some tasty Stone Island jacket you'd seen up town? Ask Mikey. You fancied some sharp gear for the kids – Gap, Next, decent stuff – have a word with Mikey. One third the price on the tag, give or take, and it was yours.

Trouble was, Mikey's reputation had been spreading a little too far and wide lately. There'd been a close one with the store detective out of David Morgan's the other week; Mikey'd lost him in the St David's Centre, but not by much, and at the time he'd thought he should give it a rest for a while. But he didn't mind going on one more little shopping trip, if that's what it took to hook Tyra up.

'What d' you want?' she said after a moment. 'You think you're going to get a little piece now my man's inside? That what you thinking, Mikey?'

Mikey put up his hands like that was the furthest thing from his mind. 'No, no. You got to pay for the clothes, you know.'

Tyra snorted and said, 'Yeah, what with?'

Mikey went on quickly, 'But no need to worry 'bout paying for it now. When's Tony gonna reach up from jail?'

Tyra stared at him. 'A year minimum, the brief says. You gonna wait a year for your money, Mikey?'

Mikey spread his hands out. 'Yeah, well. Relax, sister, we can work something out.'

'I'm not your damn sister,' said Tyra, but she didn't say anything about the working things out, let it hang there. Mikey moved in.

'I'll check you round lunchtime, OK, bring some stuff to show you.'

Tyra nodded, then walked on fast.

★   ★   ★

Mikey's shoplifting technique was a simple but effective one. Misdirection was at the heart of it. Essentially it involved him carrying on as he always did. Take this Wednesday morning. Around eleven Mikey walked into Gap. You wouldn't have thought it looked too promising – hardly any punters, two women working there, one on the till, one on the floor.

'Hiya, sweetness, how's it going?' he said to the Greek-looking girl sat behind the cash desk. 'You got a boyfriend still?'

'Yeah, and he catch you chatting me up there'd be trouble.'

'Yeah?' said Mikey. 'Yeah, well I bet he's not sweet like me. He buy you presents, girl? Let's see that chain.'

And so Nicky on the cash desk found herself pulling out the long chain her fiancé had given her for her last birthday, and then, when she caught Mikey ogling her breasts, wishing she hadn't. And so, for the rest of his time in the store, she averted her eyes from him, and acted like she was busy with some till business.

One down, one to go, thought Mikey, and moved in on the only other visible member of staff, a natural blonde about nineteen, seriously fit, who was rearranging piles of T-shirts.

'How 'bout you, darlin',' he called out. 'You got a boyfriend?'

The girl turned round, looked at Mikey, and smiled. That's what generally happened. Growing up, Mikey hadn't been too pleased to be short and bug-eyed and funny looking, but over the years he'd learned to make it work for him.

'So what do they call you, blondie?'

'Lucy,' she said.

Mikey decided to go for it straight off.

'So, Lucy,' he said, coming closer to her and affecting to

study her face, 'let me see, have you got a little Jamaican in you?'

'No,' said Lucy, bemused, evidently not a Lenny Henry fan.

'Well, any time, girl, any time!' said Mikey, cracking up as he watched Lucy put it together, and then blush furiously. A crap joke, but it worked every time. Shame his dad's people came from Anguilla, but still.

'Don't worry, girl,' he said, 'I don't bite,' at which he opened his mouth wide and then let his tongue just fraction-ally dart out. Mikey loved these uptown shop girls. Try and pull this kind of stunt in Butetown, he'd have been smacked upside the head by now. Not this Lucy, she just sort of smiled and looked at him the way you might at a cute dog that had suddenly morphed into a Doberman or something.

'So where's the kids' gear?' Mikey asked.

'Oh, right,' said Lucy and, as she started to turn round to lead him towards the back of the store, he blatantly let his eyes drop to her arse, looking nice in a pair of tight jeans. Lucy stared firmly ahead and Mikey grinned. Two out of two. From that moment on, there might as well have been a sign up – 'Help yourself, Mikey'.

And so the morning went on: Mikey's bullshit worked its magic in two out of three stores he tried. Third one, Next, it worked too well. Girl called Lorraine with a bad perm and a big bum just wouldn't leave him be, ended up making him promise to take her out on the weekend. Which was a result too. Mikey had absolutely nothing against big bums. So he was in a very good mood indeed as he headed back up to Butetown.

He made a couple of stops on the way. First in the Big

Asteys, by the bus station. Just sat at a table in the corner with a can of Pepsi Max and waited for business. Sold a couple of blouses and a pair of those kids' dungarees straight off. Took an order for a pair of Versace jeans in white and then, seeing as it was half twelve, ambled round to the Custom House.

Lot of the boys wouldn't go in the Custom House. Didn't approve of the hustlers. Even the ones didn't mind taking the girls' money, they'd still chat on about those dirty women. But Mikey was all right with the hustlers. Thing about Mikey was he really liked women, enjoyed their company a lot more than he liked going round with some bunch of geezers always making funny-ha-fucking-ha jokes about him being small and shit, treating him as some kind of mascot.

There were a couple of girls out on the street, down the side of the pub. Dayshift girls down from the valleys, doing it for their kids, like. Mikey hated the bloody valleys, full of blokes sitting round smoking draw, bollocksing on about how they used to be miners, never done a week's work between them. And all the time their wives – just off to work, dear, down the computer factory. Straight down on the train to town, outside the Custom House for the lunchtime trade. Blokes carry on pretending they didn't know. Good day on the assembly line, darlin'? Yeah, right.

Inside the pub Bobby was playing pool with some new girl, hardly looked eighteen, pretty enough, even if she'd got that white-faced 'I live on chips and speed, me' look. Mikey would have tried making a move on her if she'd been on her own, but he wasn't any too keen to go up against Bobby. A lover not a fighter, Mikey, way he saw it. Still, there were a couple more awayday girls sitting over at one of the tables by the bar, so Mikey bought a quick brandy, then went over and did a little more clothes business. One thing about hustlers, they were always ready to lay out a bit for the kids. Then he started to feel Bobby's dirty looks boring into his back and he headed out the side door.

Out in the street, he nearly bounced into a black girl called Bernice who was heading in. She was some kind of cousin of his, just got out of care.

'All right, Mikey?'

'Yeah, whassup?'

'Usual shit. You got any draw?'

'Yeah,' said Mikey, and they walked round to the car-park to spliff up, Mikey making a deal to sell her a quarter later on, when she'd made a little money.

'Listen,' he said after a moment, 'you know a girl name Tyra?'

Bernice thought for a moment. 'Y'mean the fat girl works down the health centre?'

'No,' said Mikey, 'the other one, Tyra Davies, tall girl, use to play on the basketball team, got the kids for Tony.'

Bernice nodded.

'You seen her working?' Mikey's eyes indicated the street.

'No,' said Bernice. 'Wait, I dunno, maybe someone said they'd seen her working over Riverside. Why? You looking for business?' She burst out in a peal of stoned laughter. Then, when she'd calmed down, 'You could ask Bobby.'

'Nah,' said Mikey, 'it don't matter. I'll check you later, right.'

Tyra, washing up in the kitchen, saw Mikey coming as he cut through her back yard and she had the kitchen door open before he could knock.

'What's a matter, darlin'?' said Mikey. 'Afraid the neighbours are going to see me coming round? Think you've got a little t'ing going on.'

Tyra didn't say anything, Mikey looked around him. The kitchen ran into the living-room and took up the whole ground floor. Tyra kept it tidy, he could see. Walls looked like they'd been painted recently, pictures hanging up – Robert Nesta on black velvet, big studio photo of Tony next to him. Mikey couldn't help feeling a little guilty when he looked at the photo, Tony smiling out like he didn't have a care in the world.

'Brought you some stuff,' said Mikey, moving over to the sofa in front of the TV, which was showing *Knots Landing* with the sound off. Mikey thought about asking her to turn the sound back up for a moment.

'Let's see then,' said Tyra, sitting down on the far side of the coffee table from Mikey.

Mikey brought out the gear, good stuff from Gap and Next, and even a couple of kids'-size Adidas tracksuits. When Tyra started picking the stuff up, he was sure he had her.

'So, how much?'

'For all of it?'

'Yeah.'

'Twenty,' he said, which was about half what he'd normally get for that much decent gear, but he wanted her to see what a nice guy he was.

Tyra didn't say anything for a moment. Then she sighed and said, 'OK,' and disappeared upstairs before coming back down with two tenners in her hand.

Shit, thought Mikey, wasn't supposed to go like this. 'Sure

you can spare that much, darlin'?' he said. 'Don't want to be taking the food out of your kids' mouths.'

'It's OK,' said Tyra, giving nothing away.

'You sure? You're not working, are you?'

Something flickered in Tyra's green eyes. 'What you mean, working?'

Well, this was the crunch, Mikey thought, and one of those moments when he wouldn't mind being a little bigger. Tyra had a good three inches on him, and those basketball muscles still. He moved on to the balls of his feet as he said, 'Well, I'd heard maybe you was doing a little business.'

She didn't hit him. She looked like she was thinking of spitting at him, but instead she turned away and said, 'Fuck off, Mikey. Take the money and fuck off and get your nose out of my business.'

Mikey shrugged; he wasn't a man to waste time on things that weren't working. He put his hands up. 'Easy, sister, your business is your business. But, listen, you have any trouble, you need a little management, call me, y'hear?'

Tyra kissed her teeth derisively and Mikey headed out the back, figuring that that was that then.

He spent the next week not getting much further with the career move. After an embarrassing episode outside the North Star, when some sixteen-year-old ended up hitting him with one of her shoes, he started to think that maybe he should stick with shoplifting, just do the odd awayday to Swansea or Bristol where they didn't know him.

Plus, there were more perks with the shoplifting. He'd seen that Lorraine from Next on the Saturday. Saw her down Chicago's in town so Tina wouldn't get on the warpath. Saw her again on Tuesday. Well up for it, she was. Maybe, if he left it a little while, he might get her to think about peddling a little on the side, like. She wasn't getting rich doing two days a week casual.

It was Thursday night. Mikey and Tina were just finishing off a pizza and watching some piece of shit video with Julia Roberts in it – still, worth it if it got her in the mood – when the phone rang. Luckily, she was well wrapped up in it, so it was Mikey got the phone. Tina didn't take kindly to women phoning up her husband, he had the bruises to prove it.

'Mikey,' said a woman's voice, sounding frantic.

'Yeah,' he said, wondering who the hell.

'It's Tyra.'

'Yeah,' he said again, keeping his voice gruff for Tina's benefit.

'Y'know you said you could give me some help if I needed it?'

Mikey didn't exactly remember offering help – 'management' was the word he'd used, he was pretty sure – but still he gave a vaguely affirmative grunt.

'Yeah, well I needs some help. Now, like.'

'Where are you?'

'The Four Ways.'

Mikey paused. The Four Ways was a prostitutes' pub over Riverside. Tyra must have got in a bit of bother. Taking someone else's beat, most likely. Probably some girl getting heavy with her. Well, if he was going to move into this line of business, that was the kind of shit you had to deal with.

'All right,' he said, 'I'll be right over.' She started to say something but the pips went and the phone cut out.

Tina was still watching her vid so Mikey just called out that he was stepping out for a minute – 'Bit of business.' He was out the door before the message had time to cut through Tina's focus on Julia's big love scene. Mikey wasn't too fussed, all mouth and no arse.

Down the stairs at the end of the block and into Loudoun Square, looked for the car and couldn't see it. Walked round to the Paddle Steamer, and there was cousin Del sitting outside in the motor drinking a brandy and listening to some jazz-funk tape. Mikey opened the passenger door.

'Del,' he said. 'Here's a couple of quid. Get inside the pub and get a drink. I've got to get over Riverside.'

Del, whose pupils indicated a current residence in outer space, nodded eventually, closed his hand over the money and shambled into the pub. Mikey shifted over to the driver's seat and kicked the Datsun into action.

Just as he was heading out towards Bute Street, a car flashed him. Mikey looked over to see the driver. Fucking Jim Fairfax, went to school with him over Fitzalan. Used to go down City together. Biggest damn hooligan of the lot, Jimmy Fairfax. No wonder he ended up in the police. Probably heading over the Paddle, have a couple with the boys, on the house like.

Driving over Grangetown Bridge, Mikey fingered his lock-knife as he wondered what was waiting for him over the Four Ways. Most likely some pissed-off girl from Ely with a Stanley on her, that kind of business. Well, he could handle that. 'Course there could be a pimp involved, maybe one of those Newport guys, been bringing the under-age girls over. Still, what he'd heard, they'd been chased out a week or two back, told not to come back if they didn't fancy getting Kenny's baseball bat up their arses. One thing about Kenny Ibadulla, cunt that he was, he had some standards. Well, sod it, thought Mikey, one way to find out.

He parked the car down the side of the pub, near the embankment. Hardly come to a halt when some girl in a white mini-skirt bent down to the window, asked if he was looking for business.

'No, honey, ah'm looking for love,' Mikey said in his best Eddie Murphy, and she told him to shag off and look somewhere else.

He turned the lights off and then had a quick look in the glove box, case Del had left anything there, might be useful. He smiled as his hand made contact with something, and then, held between his thumb and forefinger, he pulled out a little newspaper wrap. Del must have been so out of it he'd forgotten it. Only question was what was inside. No call for downers at a moment like this. He grinned again when he opened it up and saw white powder. Stuck in his finger and took a little taste on his tongue. Coke. Well, it could have been speed but, if Mikey had been selling, it would have been coke, all right. Either way, it was just what the doctor ordered. He speedily laid out a line on a 1978 AA yearbook he found in the passenger door, hoovered it up, put the wrap in his pocket and sauntered into the pub just as the buzz hit, ready for anything.

Well, ready for most things, anyway. He cut his eyes right as soon as he came in, towards the pool table where the hard boys hung out. Sure enough, there were a couple of the Ibadullas there, both sporting the family haircut, shaved right to the bone. They didn't look too interested in Mikey, though. One of them, Danny, raised his hand, and Mikey did likewise. He was just looking left towards where the girls usually sat when Tyra appeared right in front of him, threw her arms round him and kissed him on the mouth.

Momentarily stunned, Mikey was just about to ask where the emergency was when Tyra hissed, 'Don't say anything,' in his ear. Then she temporarily let go of him before grabbing his hand and leading him over to where she was sitting.

There were a couple of other girls around the table, Bernice and a white girl called Lynsey or something from Llanederyn, plus an older man, a guy called Charlie, used to be a boxer around when Mikey was born, had a lot of respect back then.

'All right, ladies!' said Mikey. 'How ya doing, Charlie?' ducking his head a little, making a jokey little boxing move.

'All right, man,' said Charlie, half getting up so he could reach over and tap fists with Mikey. 'All right. Now, how long you been seeing my daughter, you bad boy.'

Mikey didn't get it for a moment. He just grinned and shook his head as if responding to somebody saying something funny. Then, as he pulled up a chair, he figured it. Charlie was Tyra's old man. He supposed he'd probably always known that, but it wasn't like he'd ever lived with Tyra's mum, not since Mikey could remember, so it was hardly surprising he'd forgotten.

And then he saw the rest of it. Tyra must have been down on the beat, come in here for a warm-up with a couple of the girls, and who should she clap eyes on but her old man having a few rum and Cokes? So she must have given him some bullshit line about meeting her boyfriend here. And who should she think of but Mr Loverman himself, Mikey Dread, as they used to call him?

Mikey was both pissed off and relieved to find out that it was this kind of total foolishness that had brought him over to the Four Ways. Far as he could see, it wasn't like Charlie was in such a good state himself that he was going to pass judgement on his daughter. Can of Special outside the book-ie's, that was about what Charlie ran to these days, far as Mikey knew. Still, family was family, and anyway now he was here he might as well have a little fun.

'Yeah, man,' he said, pulling his chair right up close to Tyra and putting his hand dangerously high up on her leg, 'you got one sweet daughter here.'

Tyra let it lie for a second, then stood up and said, 'Get you a drink then, Mikey?'

'Yeah, sweetness,' he said. 'Make it a Diamond White and a brandy chaser.'

A moment later, Tyra motioned to him to give her a hand at the bar. 'Touch my leg again and you're dead,' she said.

Mikey just laughed, put his arm around her waist and pulled her to him, letting his shoulder rub against her breast. 'C'mon, darlin',' he said. 'That's not the way to talk to your new boyfriend.'

Tyra gave him one seriously cold look, and Mikey backed off a fraction. Back at the table, Bernice and Lynsey were whispering to each other and Charlie was looking at them a little askance, like he was figuring out what was really going on here.

Mikey handled it. A stream of crap jokes, lots of 'Didn't I see your auntie over town last week?' and 'How's your cousin getting on in the Rugby League there?', a string of bullshit about Prince Naz – 'You'd have taken him easy, man, easy' – to keep the old man sweet, and after half an hour or so everyone was sweet, and Mikey had his left hand practically in Tyra's knickers.

Lynsey and Bernice cried off about ten thirty, said they wanted to get home before the pubs shut. Wanted to be out on the beat for the closing-time rush, more like, but Charlie didn't seem to clock it. Instead he started talking about Mikey's dad, which Mikey thought he could do without, but was nice, really, turned out Charlie had known the old man pretty well. 'Devil for the women, ol' Lester,' he said, before looking at Mikey and Tyra and laughing.

'Damn bloody shame,' he said a little later. 'Someone should have sued the bloody shipping line.' Lester had died in some kind of accident at sea when Mikey was thirteen. This time it was Tyra who put her hand on Mikey's knee.

It was half midnight before they finally made it out of the pub. Charlie was three sheets to the wind by then, so Tyra put him in a minicab back to Ely.

Mikey and Tyra walked round to the car. There were still a couple of girls out. No sign of Bernice, but Lynsey was there smoking a fag and looking cold. Tyra stopped for a quick word and Mikey walked round to unlock the car. He got into the driver's seat, then leaned over to open the door for Tyra.

As he did so, he saw a bloke walk up, an obvious punter. He looked quickly at Tyra and Lynsey then said something to Tyra. Mikey couldn't hear what exactly, but it wasn't hard to figure. Tyra looked round, caught Mikey's eyes.

Mikey looked back. But he couldn't say anything. In the end he bottled out. His big pimp chance gone. He called to Tyra, 'C'mon, doll.' She walked to the car, smiling. The punter walked off, shaking his head. Lynsey walked after the punter, shouting out something.

'Mikey,' said Tyra, 'you're all right.'

Mikey just inclined his head slightly and started driving, but he felt good. Felt even better when they got back to Tyra's. Even when Tina gave him a serious beating after he got home at four in the morning, left him with a bleeding nose and a couple of ribs he'd have sworn were broken, he still felt good.

Shit, he thought, as he lay there on the sofa, wondering how bad he was going to hurt in the morning, he might not be much of a villain, but he certainly got a lot of action for a little guy.

The Packet

Monday morning, and Kim had a headache. She was sitting in the weekly ideas meeting and, to be honest, she was feeling like shit. Mostly it was a hangover; why anyone had parties on a Sunday night, she couldn't imagine. She didn't have the ghost of an idea for the meeting and it was going to be her turn next. Still, she'd been in the job three months now and they hadn't looked twice at any of the ideas she'd come up with so far, so big deal, really.

'Kim,' said Huw, the director. 'Any thoughts? Or should I fetch you a couple of paracetamol?'

'No thanks,' she said, thinking 'bastard'. She was doing her best to fancy Huw; it was part of the makeover she was trying to effect on her so-called life. She'd started wearing black all the time; that was a given, if you were going to be a media chick. She'd had her long wavy brown hair cut short, bobbed and hennaed. She'd stopped wearing heels so she didn't tower over her midget boss. Her accent was getting snottier and less Cardiff every day, so her mam said, and now she was working on upgrading her class of boyfriend. No more PT instructors. That was her New Year's resolution. But, God knows, jerks like Huw weren't making it easy.

'So, Kim? What have you got for us? Any tales from Cardiff clubland to follow up? Sex, drugs, rock and roll – that kind of thing?'

Kim closed her eyes for a moment. Opened them again pretty quickly when everything swirled about behind her eyelids. And in her brain too, come to that.

'Drugs,' she said all of a sudden.

'Sorry, Kim,' said Huw, 'can't oblige, I'm afraid. Paracetamol's best I can do.' He turned round to his pals, Sian the producer and a scary woman named Anne whose job Kim hadn't yet figured out, and they laughed dutifully.

Which suited Kim fine, as in that instant something popped into her brain.

'Cocaine wars,' she said.

'What?' said Huw.

'Yeah,' said Kim, dredging her memory for a conversation her mate had been having with some bloke at God knows what time the night before. 'What I've heard is there's this kind of turf war, yeah, between these cocaine dealers down the docks and some people from out of town.'

'Really,' said Huw, and looked round to his cronies with his eyebrows raised, but swivelled back again quickly when he saw that Sian's attention was firmly focused on Kim.

'Great,' said Sian, 'that sounds really interesting.'

Kim was excited. No point in pretending not to be. She'd slaved in the PR department, brown-nosing every twat that passed in front of her, for too long not to be excited, now she'd finally got her break as a researcher on *Wednesday Week*. With a chance to present too, if the right story came along. That's what they said at the interview, anyway, believe it when she saw it. And now maybe she'd finally got it. The right idea.

Huw popped out of his office and over to her cubicle just before lunch. 'Kim,' he said, 'this drugs-war thing. You know it's all a load of bullshit, don't you?'

'What?' she said.

'Yeah,' he said, 'I've got a couple of very good sources in the police. They keep me informed if anything's going on.'

'Oh,' she said. 'Well, it's just what I . . .'

Huw held his hand up. 'Yes, yes, I'm sure, but people do talk a lot of crap in nightclubs, don't they?'

Apparently that was it. Huw turned round and headed for his office. Kim couldn't resist flicking a V-sign at the back of his Next blazer as it disappeared down the corridor. She only just got her fingers down in time as he spun round again and said, 'Don't look so disappointed, dear. Tell you what, I'll just call one of my sources, check there's nothing in it.'

Ten minutes later, Huw came out again, his coat on now on top of his blazer.

'Well,' he said to Kim, 'I've had a word with my contacts and, you know what, you may be on to something. Fancy coming for lunch?'

And that's how it started.

It was his brief told Mikey about the documentary. Said he'd had a call from some bloke on *Wednesday Week*, the BBC thing.

'Wants to know all about the drugs war, Mikey.'

Mikey laughed, so did the brief, Terry – Mr Richards – who was a decent bloke all in all, down to earth, like, and had one lovely receptionist, Donna, which meant that Mikey didn't mind walking into town even for a little matter like this one. Some bollocks about wanting him to testify in court. One of the hustlers said he was a witness to some foolishness with a knife, happened outside the North Star a couple of weeks back.

'Drugs war, Terry? You heard of any drugs war?'

Terry shook his head. 'Huw, the TV bloke, sounded serious about it, though. Someone gave him Kenny's name, told him Kenny's going to war with some Birmingham Yardies, and they're all excited.'

Mikey raised his eyebrows, didn't comment.

'Anyway, they're looking for someone from the docks to help them out, be their researcher. Show 'em the lie of the land.'

Mikey raised his eyebrows again. 'Money in it, Terr?'

Terry shrugged. 'I'm not your agent, Mikey. The TV guy's name is Huw. Huw Jarvis. Now, what's this North Star business about?'

'Nothing, Terry, believe me, couple of girls got a bit aereated outside the club, Tina got a knife out, the other girl, don't even know her name, had a Stanley in her bag. Tina got a little cut on her arm, bled all over the place, fat as she is.'

'What's that, Mikey, girls fighting over you again?' The voice came from behind him, Donna bringing in a pile of papers.

'That's right, darlin',' he said, 'they don't like me seeing so much of you.'

Donna kissed her teeth. 'Well, feast your eyes, Mikey, 'cause this is all you're seeing.'

Ten minutes later, Mikey was back on the street and in a good mood. Terry had told what he already knew – sit tight and the odds of the court case coming off were practically nil. The last thing any of the girls wanted to do was sit around all day in court when they could be out earning a living. Then Donna had turned him down three times for a drink, but that was all right too. Mikey was a great believer in the drip-drip theory of seduction.

He didn't think about the TV guy again till late on in the evening having a quiet game of pool down the Avondale with a couple of the valleys boys, come down to pick up some supplies for Col. Skunk was going through the roof. Couldn't get enough of it in Ponty, by all accounts.

Col didn't even show till half eleven, which was typical. Lucky it was the Avondale; just had to knock on the side door and you were in for as long as you or Bryn the barman could hack it. Anyway, Col had the merchandise, which calmed down the valleys boys. One of them rolled up a sampler straight off, which was another user-friendly feature of the Avondale.

'Shit,' said Col a little while later, after the valleys boys had saddled up their ancient Sierra and headed home.

'What?' said Mikey.

'That's the end of the skunk for this year. 'Cept mi personal supplies, like. Got to find another little job.'

'Don't Kenny have anything for you?'

'Nah, little bit of door here, bit of bar there. 'Less I want to get into his gangster business and I'm getting too old for that shit.'

Mikey nodded in sympathy, then thought of something. 'How d'you fancy working for a TV company?'

Col just looked at him, like he was waiting for the punch-line, but Mikey carried on and told him about what Terry had said. When he finished Col said, 'Yeah. Let's have a laugh with them.'

Next lunchtime, around two o'clock, there they all were sitting round a table at the back of the Packet. Mikey and Col, and Huw and Kim from the TV, three of them on the Labatt's, Huw on the Brains Light.

They'd been sat there for half an hour or so. Col had hardly said a word, just sat back looking moody while Mikey rattled out his usual bullshit, probably have had his tongue in Kim's ear if he'd sat any closer to her. Finally, in the microscopic pause between a couple of Mikey's stories, Huw leaned forward and said in a half whisper, 'Is it safe to talk?'

Col nearly burst out laughing. There wasn't a soul within twenty feet of them, and the boys hardly ever used the Packet anyway, that's why they'd picked it for the meet. But Mikey was evidently made of sterner stuff, and he made a show of looking around the pub cautiously before starting to talk very quietly so that everyone else had to lean forward, and, in Kim's case, brush up next to him.

'So,' he said, 'you people have heard about the drugs war we're having down here.'

'Well,' said Huw, looking pleased to be such an in-the-know sort of cat, 'we've heard some rumours . . .'

'Rumours,' said Mikey. 'What sort of rumours?'

Huw looked around even more carefully, like he thought someone might be bugging the fireplace. 'We've heard Kenny Ibadulla's involved.'

Mikey nodded seriously, as if every kid in kindergarten didn't know Kenny Ibadulla was a gangster.

'And the Yardies,' added Kim, smiling like she was the goose laying the golden egg, and Mikey turned to give her a big grin as if she'd said something really on the button. Yardies! Fucking hell. Put any three black guys together on the street after lunchtime and, far as Mr and Mrs General Public were concerned, you had a gang of Yardies. Never mind the closest they've been to Jamaica's a day trip down Porthcawl.

'Yeah,' he said, 'there's some well heavy geezers around. Isn't it, Col?'

Col's attention had been elsewhere, fighting the urge to nip outside and fire up some skunk, leave these idiots to it. So he just nodded and instinctively repeated Mikey's words. 'Well heavy,' he said.

The table fell silent for a moment as everyone present ruminated on the heaviness of Yardies.

'So where've you been hearing this?' asked Mikey.

Huw and Kim looked at each other, and Huw was just starting to say something about sources and confidentiality when Kim cut in and said, 'The police. We had a briefing from the chief constable. He's worried about, quote, Cardiff becoming a major staging post on the cocaine trail, unquote.'

This provoked Col and Mikey to look at each other. Mikey raised his eyebrows and Col shrugged in a 'search me' kind of way.

'Look,' said Mikey. 'You got any idea what you're getting on to here?'

Huw and Kim nodded, rather nervously.

' 'Cause, like I say, there are some well heavy geezers involved. Innit, Col?'

Col nodded microscopically while staring heavy-lidded at the TV people, as if measuring them for toughness. Then he suddenly leaned forward. 'Tell you what, you say you want to do this thing proper?'

Huw and Kim nodded again, both feeling slightly foolish and increasingly out of their depth.

'Right,' said Col. 'Best thing, you go undercover. You got some expenses?'

'Mmm,' said Kim. Huw was about to wade in with some sort of mealy-mouthed qualification but Col cut him off.

'OK, we'll set you up with a buy. Everyone knows you media people like a bit of Charlie, yeah. So we'll see you in the Cantonese over Riverside, nine o'clock tonight, all right. And no camera business, yeah. This is just the start.'

And, before Huw or Kim could say anything, he stood up and Mikey did likewise.

'See you at nine,' said Mikey to Kim, holding on to her hand a good couple of seconds too long.

'All right,' said Kim, flustered, looking at Huw for some kind of sign that it would be all right.

Nine o'clock. Mikey, Col, Col's baby mother Maria, and Mikey's mate Darren, who was just back from a little sojourn down Dartmoor, were all sat in the front bar of the Tudor Arms, smack opposite the Cantonese. Around ten past a rather tasty-looking Honda Accord drew up outside the restaurant and out come Huw and Kim. They both looked around warily, as if they were going to spot a bunch of Brummie Yardies waiting in ambush, then ducked into the restaurant.

'Give 'em half an hour to start shitting it,' said Mikey, and the others laughed, though in fact it was only about ten minutes before Maria said she was bloody starving and Col said he was too and all, and they headed over the road.

Inside the Cantonese, the head-waiter guy gave them a bit of a look till one of the other waiters came up to Col and said, 'All right, butt.'

Col said, 'Yeah, how's it going, Ricky,' and clashed fists with the guy, much to the head-waiter's disapproval.

Mikey caught Kim's eye. She was sat over at a corner table as far away from the window as possible. She raised her hand in a small wave. Mikey walked over and ushered her and Huw to a big round table slap in front of the window. Col ordered up a top-of-the-line set meal for everybody. Peking duck, crispy seaweed, the whole works. He gave a meaningful nod towards Huw as he did so. Huw correctly interpreted the nod as meaning 'this one's on the BBC', and did his best to look relaxed as he nodded back.

Meanwhile Mikey started making the introductions. Maria he introduced as Maria. Darren, however, he introduced as 'um, Paulo', leaving no one in any doubt that this was not in fact his real name. Darren looked about as much like a Paulo as Cardiff City looked like Barcelona.

For the first half hour or so, conversation was a little strained. The TV duo were nervous, Col was his usual low-key self, Darren seemed completely freaked by the whole situation, and Maria was still pissed off with Mikey over a little misunderstanding outside the Custom House a while back. So it was left to Mikey to single-handedly keep things going.

After a couple of rounds of lager, things livened up a bit and Mikey finally scored a hit when he asked Kim if the things people said about a couple of daytime TV presenters were true. So Kim took the chance to deliver a few choice nuggets of TV-world gossip. That and the Peking duck being passed round, and soon you could almost have mistaken the table for a social gathering.

Then, as the last traces of pancake, plum jam and duck were being mopped up, Col leaned over to Huw and said quietly,

'Give Kim there a ton, tell her to follow Maria into the toilet next time she goes. She's the one.'

'Maria?'

Col nodded.

'Not Paulo?'

Col widened his eyes in a disgusted kind of way and leant even closer to Huw. 'Paulo isn't going to be holding, is he? He's only been out of Dartmoor for a week.'

Huw nodded quickly, then he turned away, tapped Kim on the shoulder and made a spectacularly clumsy job of surreptitiously passing her the money while whispering in her ear.

A couple of minutes later Maria headed for the ladies', and Kim, as instructed by Huw, followed suit. After ten minutes the two women emerged. You didn't need a sniffer dog to suspect that they might have been having a little tasting session back there.

Next morning, Kim had another serious hangover. She counted her blessings first. She was in her own bed, by herself. She was indubitably alive, or her head wouldn't be hurting so much, and she'd made sure he'd used a condom, so she didn't have to worry. Whether that was a blessing or just a not-curse, she couldn't quite decide. Well, in her state, she felt you took blessings where you could find them.

She'd done it with Mikey, of course. She supposed she'd known she was going to. She'd fancied Col a lot more, from the off, but you could tell that Mikey was the one who'd put the work in. Col she'd have had to chase and, to give her her due, she wasn't reduced to that yet. Mikey started chasing the moment he clapped eyes on her, and by four o'clock in the morning, or whatever time it had been they got back to that flat – Maria's, she supposed it was – well, she didn't like to see a man put in that much running for nothing.

And it had been fun, she thought, what she remembered of it. God, weren't drugs great! She looked at the clock, saw it was still only eight o'clock, figured that the only reason she didn't feel worse than she did was that she must still be half cut, and decided to take another half-hour's nap. She curled up, her hand between her legs, and was just drifting off when she was assailed by the memory of a nipple between her lips. For a moment, she thought it was just some kind of student flashback, but then the image broadened out and suddenly she was lying on her front, biting the pillow and thumping her fist against the mattress as she shook with laughter. Maria and her in Maria's surprisingly big, nice bathroom, snorting up a couple of huge lines of coke off the edge of the bath, then all of a sudden snogging each other. And stuff.

'And stuff – you dirty cow,' Kim said to herself, and then, once again, aren't drugs great! With that, she turned over again, and next thing she knew it was a quarter to ten and she was an hour late for work, but what the hell. Her hangover seemed to have disappeared and she felt totally bloody excellent.

She was still feeling fine at eleven oh five when she finally made it to the BBC offices out in Llandaff North. Felt fine as Jo on reception took the piss. Felt fine as she got a cup of coffee from the machine and sat down in her blissfully quiet cubicle with the *Western Mail*. Didn't feel quite so fine five minutes later when Huw came out of his office, sat down right opposite her and just gave her this look. Kind of look that had her wanting to check there wasn't a white stain on her skirt or a little bit of coke crusted under her nose.

'So,' he said, 'somebody had a good time last night.'

Kim didn't say anything, waiting to see how Huw wanted to play it.

'Well, you're sure you're not too exhausted after your exertions . . .' Huw tailed off. Kim could see he was dying to ask her just what she had got up to. Meanwhile she was desperately trying to remember how long he'd stuck around. After the meal they'd all piled into Huw's car and driven back down the docks. Gone down the Casablanca first. All of them nipping in and out of the toilets every ten minutes. All except Huw, of course; BBC producers on a fast track couldn't take that kind of risk but, fair play to him, he'd turned a blind eye.

After the Casa closed, around two, Col had suggested they all go round to Kenny Ibadulla's place – Black Caesar's – said it'd be open another hour or so, be a good chance to get their faces seen around town. She thought she could remember Huw being there then – but she couldn't remember him leaving. All she could remember about Caesar's was dancing with Mikey, trying to do some kind of a ragga move, Mikey round behind her, rubbing up against her bum, obviously very pleased to see her. Shit, she hoped Huw had gone by then.

And then, with a sudden flash of hungover genius, she spotted that the best form of defence of her conduct had got to be attack.

'Huw,' she said, leaning forward, 'you should have stuck around. Just wait till you hear what I found out.'

Huw raised his eyebrows.

'I know when the next big shipment's coming into town.'

'Uh, huh.' Bastard doing his best not to look impressed.

'Yeah, it'll be coming by boat.'

'Yeah?'

'Yeah.'

'That's not it, is it, Kim? I think we could all figure out that a boat is the best way of bringing stuff into Cardiff Docks. Your sources happen to mention which boat?'

'Mmm,' said Kim, desperately trying to think where boats might come from into Cardiff. Then she shook her head. 'No, it's gone. I just can't remember anything with this hangover.'

She thought Huw was about to explode as she waited a couple of seconds before carrying on. 'Do me a favour, Huw, and stop looking at me like you've never seen a person with a hangover before. Of course I can remember which boat it is.'

Huw forced a grin on to his face and said, 'Sorry, Kim.'

'Yeah, well,' she said, 'the boat is coming from . . .' Suddenly she remembered a boat story she'd worked on back when she first started on the show. 'The boat's coming from St Helena.'

Even as the words were out of her mouth, she started to regret them. As far as she could remember, St Helena was in the middle of absolutely bloody nowhere.

'St Helena,' said Huw, a note not quite of incredulity but definitely of surprise in his voice. 'Isn't that in the middle of nowhere?'

'Yeah . . . that's the whole point. Apparently it's like a crossroads between Africa and South America and that, and no one expects anything to be coming in from there. All the boats from the West Indies and stuff are more dangerous to use.'

'Oh,' said Huw. 'Right. Makes sense, I guess. So how often do the boats run?'

Kim knew the answer to this one. 'Every three months. Twenty days' sailing time.'

'Christ,' said Huw, starting to look excited. 'So d'you know how they smuggle it in? Not that it matters at this stage.'

'Tuna,' said Kim, 'big tins of tuna. It's about the only thing they export.'

So, a little later that afternoon, Kim found herself a quiet little office and settled down to make some phone calls, one to the lawyer, Terry Richards, to get Mikey's number. One to Mikey, which got a very frosty reception from a woman with the strongest Cardiff accent Kim had ever heard in all her years of living in the city. Then one to the Avondale where, it had grudgingly been conceded, Mikey might be. No joy there, though, and Kim was starting to sweat, wondering what would happen if Huw got hold of Mikey or Col first, asked them about St bloody Helena.

Col. She couldn't believe she was being so dumb. She dug around in her bag till she found a scrap of paper with a mobile number on it.

Col answered straight away and she set up a meet in the Packet, six o'clock. Then she went to see Huw, put him off coming. That was easy enough. He was busy filling forms in triplicate justifying the money he'd spent already, and was happy enough to stay out when she told him it would be better if she went on her own. They'd talk more in front of a woman, they'll let things slip to me, things they wouldn't if you were around. Huw nodded seriously, and told her to be careful.

Mikey was the first into the pub. Getting out past Tina had been a nightmare. He'd come in from doing a little bit of business around four, picked little Mikey up from school on the way. The second little Mikey was sat in front of his programmes, she'd started in. Some posh tart had phoned up for him, said she was from the BBC, how stupid did he think she was, like the fucking BBC would be phoning you up.

'Calm down, woman,' Mikey said, 'it's the truth. Terry gave her my number. I told you yesterday.'

'Yeah, and I believed you. Like a twat. Then you come in at five in the fucking morning.'

Bollocks, Mikey thought. He was sure he'd got in without her noticing the time. Now he knew whatever he said there was going to be trouble.

'Yeah, well,' he said. 'They wanted to go down Kenny's club, check out the scene, y'know what I mean?'

Tina looked at Mikey for a moment, standing there in the kitchen while she made some cheese on toast for her son, smiling this bullshit smile at her, and she snapped. Threw the frying pan straight at him and, when he dodged left to get out of the way of it, she caught him with a kick to the shin and whipped her fingernails hard across his cheek, feeling them cut into the flesh.

'Fuck,' said Mikey, and 'fuck' again as he raised his hand to his cheek and found wetness there. Tina just stood stock still, transfixed for a moment by the sight of the blood on Mikey's cheek. He seized the chance to shake his head and say you're well out of order and scarper to the bathroom.

Spot of Savlon on the cuts and a couple of minutes getting his hair right, and he came out cautiously. When Tina didn't immediately return to the attack, he reckoned she must be feeling guilty so he walked into the kitchen. He found her standing next to the cooker crying, the smell of burnt cheese pervading the air.

'I'm going out,' he said. 'TV business.'

Sitting with his brandy at the bar of the Packet, he thought to himself that he had to stop letting women beat him up. Second time in a fortnight this was: first his girlfriend, now his wife. He'd mentioned to Lorraine, the girl from Next, that she might like to try using her talents in the pro leagues. And she'd responded with one hell of a straight right that made him wonder if she might not have a real sporting future, if they ever get women's boxing off the ground proper. Women were his Achilles' heel, he couldn't help feeling.

On which note Kim walked in. He let her buy him another brandy, a Labatt's for herself, shaking her head saying it had been a hell of a day.

Then she looked at Mikey properly, ready to say something nice about what had happened the night before, but instead came out with, 'What the hell happened to your face?'

Mikey put his hand up to his cheek, laughed and said, 'You should see the other guy.'

Kim laughed and said, 'Yeah, I certainly should. Must have some set of fingernails. You been fighting with a transvestite then?'

Mikey looked at her hard for the first time, gave her a real look, the one he gave people who lived in his world. She held it, looked straight back at him. Mikey cracked first, started laughing, then she laughed too. Kim, he decided, was cool.

He was convinced of it when they sat down at the back of the pub and she told him what she'd told Huw, especially when she got to the punchline.

'St Helena?' he said. 'You told him St Helena?' and he started to laugh.

'Yeah,' she said, grinning herself.

'And he went for it?'

'Yeah,' she said, now laughing too. 'Hook, line and bloody sinker.'

Just then Col arrived, clashed fists with Mikey, nodded to Kim. She didn't think Col liked her much. Mikey seemed oblivious, though.

'St Helena, Col,' he repeated. 'Isn't that the funniest fucking thing you ever heard? There's only the one boat ever goes there, coming or going. They'd have to smuggle the stuff there, then smuggle it back out again.'

Col did his best to look unamused but after a few seconds a smile broke out and he sat down.

'Well,' he said. 'So how's that fit into your drugs war, then?'

'Oh,' said Kim, 'that's what we're paying you guys for, tell us things like that.'

It was Col's turn now to look long and hard at Kim. 'So you've sold your boss some bullshit about this gear coming in from St Helena and now you want us to tell you some bullshit about how that fits into this drugs war?'

Kim nodded, let a smile start to show on her face.

'This drugs war, right,' Col went on. 'You know it's all crap?'

Kim nodded again.

'But I don't suppose that matters to you TV people – whether it's crap or not?'

Kim nodded yet again but Col carried on.

'Leastwise,' he said. 'I don't reckon you mind whether it's

kosher or not. Your boss Huw, he probably cares, right?' He waited for Kim's nod. 'But if we set up a little situation that looked good on film, he probably wouldn't ask too many questions, right?'

The St Helena boat came in at ten o'clock on a Sunday night. The next morning Tony the cameraman was in place at six, hiding out in an old warehouse, his long lens trained on the boat. Around half past eleven, he'd just got off his mobile for the third time, telling Huw to call him back to the office, he had better things to do than freeze his bollocks off out here. That's when he saw the two guys he'd been told about, a tall Rasta and a short guy.

Tony got the footage of the two of them walking on to the boat, and half an hour later he got them coming off again. This time the short guy was carrying a holdall and he seemed to be laughing. Tony whistled to himself at the arrogance of the guy. Walking off a boat in plain daylight carrying God knows how much coke in a holdall and laughing about it. He started tingling, knowing full well how good the tight close-up he was getting would look. A shame, though, he thought, that they had no way of picking up what the guys were saying to each other.

'Christ,' Col was saying to Mikey, 'stop bloody smiling. You're supposed to have a load of coke in the bag, you should look like you're shitting yourself.'

'Yeah, sorry, Col,' said Mikey, and shifted the holdall from one hand to the other, trying to make it look heavy.

Later on they filmed a bit more round Col's brother's place, a couple of the boys done up as Yardies – gold, big trainers, dark glasses – and that was it, a done deal. One of those times everybody's happy. Kim forked over the expenses to Mikey and Col, and back in the editing suite she was well and truly belle of the ball.

'Remarkable documentary footage,' somebody said and everyone agreed.

'And no questions asked,' said Huw, tapping the side of his nose.

Kim looked him straight in the eye and he held the look. Maybe he wasn't such a bad bloke after all, she thought.

The Paddle Steamer

Mandy liked a little drama in her life. It was the only way she could explain it, stupid situations she'd get herself into. Not that this wasn't the best yet. Leaving Neville to go out with a cop, for Christ's sake. And now they were both going to be coming down the Paddle tonight, listen to her playing records.

'What d'you reckon I should do, Linz?' she asked, sitting round the childminder's having a cup of tea and a smoke, ten o'clock that morning.

'Leave the bloody country, love,' said Linsey, big and florid and bottle-blonde, where Mandy was wiry and neat, her naturally wavy dirty-blonde hair drawn back tightly into a short ponytail. Then she spluttered with laughter, looking at Mandy's crestfallen face. 'Nah, leave 'em to it. Jimmy can look after himself.'

'It's not Jimmy I'm worried about. It's Neville. He starts giving Jimmy grief . . .'

Linsey shook her head. 'You're right, he was always mental, Jimmy Fairfax. Remember at school?'

Mandy laughed too, didn't say anything.

'Seriously, though, love,' Linsey went on. 'Why don't you?'

'Why don't I what?'

'Leave the country. Go and stay with your dad. He sounds well set up over there.'

Mandy stiffened slightly, as she tried to remember what she'd told Linsey about her dad lately. Usually she said he was in Florida. She always said he'd made his money in the construction business, she knew she stuck to that, but the other day she'd been watching some vid with a couple of mates, set in Los Angeles, and she'd suddenly come out with it, 'Oh, my dad lives there.' Silly cow she was. Still, maybe he could have two homes, one in Florida, one in LA. That sounded good.

'Yeah, well,' she said, 'I've got my responsibilities here, you know . . .'

Just then Linsey's little boy, Jordan, whacked Mandy's youngest, Emma, in the back, sending her tumbling towards the TV. Linsey plunged forward just in time to stop her putting her head through the screen but not soon enough to stop her bursting into explosive screams, and Mandy decided it was time to go.

'Ta-ra now, Linz,' she said, putting her mug down by the sink and nipping out the back door before the childminder had a chance to say anything.

Back out on the street, she checked her watch. Still only quarter past ten, plenty of time to walk down Spiller's, pick up a couple of singles before she had to be in the pub at twelve. Cope with the lunchtime rush. Ha ha.

Walking down the back way, along Angelina Street, she started to worry again. Jimmy Fairfax, what in hell's name was she doing with Jimmy Fairfax?

It had started a couple of months ago. She'd finally had it with Nev, taken off with the kids down her sister's in Newport. Stayed there for a couple of weeks, giving Nev time to cool off, like, then she'd come back to Butetown.

Moved in with her mum down the bottom there. And after a couple of days she'd gone back to work, left the kids with Linz, all just like before except no Nev giving her grief.

Then, Friday afternoon after the lunch shift, she goes to pick up the kids and they're not there. Linz says, 'Oh, Neville came and picked them up.' Stupid cow just went and let him.

'Course she'd completely freaked. It was embarrassing, really. She'd had a couple of brandies over lunchtime and, anyway, next thing she knew she was calling up the local TV, saying her kids had been kidnapped and their dad was going to smuggle them out of the country.

Must have been a quiet day or something 'cause in no time they had her up in the studio pleading for the public to help her get her kids back. She hadn't been meaning to get the police involved, just wanted to freak Nev out, basically, but the TV people called them in anyway, and she couldn't believe it who should they send up the studio to talk to her. Fucking Jimmy Fairfax. Last time she remembered having anything to do with him, they'd both been sent out of class – different classes, she'd never been that thick – and he'd tried to feel her tits in the corridor. Twat. But, fifteen years later, she had to admit he'd changed.

Anyway, she'd gone for it when they got to the studio. Tears, the whole bit, and they'd done a nice job with the make-up and all, and Jimmy had gone on after her, appealing for anyone who knew where the kids might be to phone in. Then, after she'd been waiting for the TV people to call her a cab, Jimmy said he'd drop her back down, said he was living in one of the new places over the marina there.

So they were chatting a bit in his car – one of those Mazda 323s – and she had to say she fancied him like hell. So they were almost back down the docks when she gave it another bit of the old waterworks, said she couldn't face being alone, would he mind going for a drink with her, keep her company for a little bit. So they went down the Wharf there on the marina, which should have been no problem except it was only Leanne's sister behind the bar, gave them a bit of a look.

Still, they were only having a drink and she was a free woman, wasn't she, and after a couple she was telling Jimmy how much she appreciated his support and she had her hand on his leg and she reckoned he was getting the message, except she looked at the clock and saw it was ten past eight and she should have been in work at half seven. So he drops her back over the Paddle and gives her his phone number – let him know if there are any developments, like – and she says ta and walks in the pub and there's Neville and the kids waiting for her, Neville looking like blue bloody murder.

So, anyway, next day she'd given Jimmy a bell and told him she'd got the kids back, gave him some bollocks about catching them at Neville's cousin's place with the passports all ready and everything. And then she started crying, telling him how Neville had slapped her and all – which he had, though nothing much. So Jimmy had been all concerned and he'd come round to see her and she had a nice big bruise on her cheek, she always bruised easy, and he'd asked her if she wanted him to sort the bastard out and she'd said no but gave him a bit of a hug and, well, one thing had led to a bit of the other, really.

It had been going on for a month or so now. She hadn't meant it to, but the thing was, Jimmy was just so bloody keen on her that . . . Well, it drove her mad, really, but still she liked it, Christ knows she'd had little enough of that with Nev the last couple of years. Jimmy was mad for her so . . .

The main thing was she'd kept it from Neville so far. Bruise he'd given her the last time would be nothing what'd happen he found out about Jimmy. Not that Jimmy couldn't sort him out – Jimmy had muscles on his muscles – but that would be that then, restraining orders and all that. Most likely have to move out her flat. And she'd be stuck with Jimmy big time then, and frankly she wasn't sure about that at all. Not at all. And, far as she could see, she'd better make her mind up by tonight. Shit, she thought, why can't life be a little more simple? And she was just cursing her luck when she realised she had a dirty great smile on her face. She couldn't help it. Like she said, she was a right old drama queen.

She spent half an hour in Spiller's chatting up the bloke with the long hair and picking up some chart stuff for the disco. Spiller's was the best place for that; must be a chart return shop, she reckoned, they had all the special offers. Then she went down the arcade to pick up a couple of house tunes, even though she doubted there'd be much demand, crowd she'd be playing to tonight.

The rest of the day was pure same old same old – work in the pub, pick the kids up from Linz, give them their tea, took them round her mum's for the night, back home, quick change and cart her records over the Paddle.

By nine o'clock she was enjoying herself, pumping out some solid house tunes, smoking some serious skunk, just her and a couple of mates in the back bar so far. 'Course she knew it was the lull before the storm and all, but she was enjoying it anyway.

It was Neville showed up first, around ten, and it could

hardly have been worse. He came in with Kenny and Col. Neville on the right, Col on the left, like a pair of bookends with Kenny in the middle. Kenny was really the last person she wanted to see in this situation. Not that she didn't get on with him all right. He was some kind of cousin of hers and he'd always looked out for her when they were kids, even though he was a few years older and all, but the thing about Kenny was he really hated the police. Just the sight of Jimmy would get him going. Let alone finding out Jimmy was knocking off his mate's woman. Way he would see it, she knew. Nothing for it, she had to get rid of them.

First thing she thought of was driving them out with music. She knew Kenny was like her when it came to music, took it serious. A lot of the boys were still living in the past when it came to tunes – play the Gap Band all night, they'd be happy – but Kenny was house and garage all the way. Well, she hated to do it but there was nothing else for it, so she dug under the table she had the decks on and found the box of singles she kept for children's parties, and there it was, right at the front. 2 Unlimited.

Whoa oh. Whoa whoa oh oh there's no limit.

Perfect, a whole bunch of people drifted on to the dance floor, unable to resist the Pavlovian simplicity of the beat. Normally that would piss Mandy off royally, like playing records to a bunch of sheep, but this time she had her whole attention focused on Kenny and his face had turned gratifyingly dark.

Then, bollocks, Col leaned over to say something to Kenny and he started laughing and they just stood there at the bar chatting away as the record played. Neville even gave her a smile and a wave. Shit, she thought, and dug deep into the kiddy record box, flicking through the records furiously before her eyes seized on something.

And so 2 Unlimited's floor-filling 'No Limit' was followed by Culturebeat's likewise floor-filling 'Mr Vain', and this time Kenny could take it no longer. He walked over to the decks.

'All right, Mand,' he said. 'What are you playing this shit for?'

Mandy just shook her head. 'I know, Ken, I know.' Then she shrugged in the direction of the heaving dance floor and said, 'But what can you do, Ken? They love this shit, and Peter told me to give them what they want.'

This was bollocks, of course; Peter the landlord wouldn't know 2 Unlimited from James Brown, but Kenny seemed to buy it. 'Yeah, well,' he said, 'I better be going down the club. See you later, Mand.'

Mandy just smiled and said, 'Yeah, later, Ken.'

The big man headed back to the bar, collected Col, and was gone before the track finished. Mandy just managed to restrain herself from whipping it off the second she saw his broad back pass through the door.

An hour later there was still no sign of Jimmy, and Mandy was feeling pretty relaxed about things, so relaxed that when Neville came over while she was playing some Mary J. Blige tune, and asked her if she fancied a dance, she said, 'Yeah, why not.' And, without even thinking about it, she started rubbing up against him as they moved, letting the music take over.

Later still, five to midnight, last tune of the night, just like always, Phyllis Nelson's 'Move Closer' – didn't finish with that in the Paddle, you were dead meat – Neville was taking the words to heart. Moved any closer, she'd be in serious danger of pregnancy. Well, she wouldn't actually; after her youngest, Brittany, was born she'd gone down the clinic got herself a coil. No way you could trust the docks boys to use a condom: like standing in the shower with your coat on, Neville used to say. Wanker, but, still, right now, him holding her tight, she couldn't help remembering why she liked him in the first place.

She closed her eyes for a second, let everything go but the moment. Then she opened them again, thinking it'd be just her luck if Jimmy Fairfax came in right now.

He didn't, though. Didn't turn up even when she was packing the records away, and getting ready to go. No, what he did was he rang on her bell, half past one in the morning, her and Neville lying in bed together having a friendly fag, like, after giving each other a fair-old going-over.

Ding bloody dong went the door chime which normally she liked, spent ages in Do It All testing out the different rings.

'Who the fuck's that?' said Neville.

'No one I wants to see,' said Mandy.

'You want me to go down, tell 'em to fuck off?'

'No, leave it, Nev, they'll piss off in a minute.'

But the bell rang again, and then again, and Mandy, sighing, got out of bed and pulled a big T-shirt on. Neville started to get up too, but Mandy motioned to him to stay put. 'Could be the law, I don't want them knowing my business.'

Neville nodded.

Downstairs, Mandy opened the door, saw Jimmy Fairfax standing there just as large as grief, put her finger to her lips before he could say anything and smartly ushered him into the front room.

Five more seconds of her standing there like a lemon,

absolutely unable to think of anything sensible to say, he obviously thinks she's playing some kind of game and he's over to her. Mouth on her mouth, freezing cold hands up the back of her T-shirt, pushing the whole T-shirt up above her waist, pushing her towards the sofa, like they're going to do it right here and now. Idiot's been watching too many videos.

'Stop it,' she said, attempting to giggle very quietly. 'The kids.'

'Kids are fast asleep, Mand,' he said, 'come on,' and went back on the attack, biting her neck now. She wasn't sure whether to laugh or knee him in the balls. Part of her even thought, sod it, what the hell.

But then, all of a sudden, he stopped of his own accord, shot bolt upright and stood back a pace, letting go of Mandy in the process. Mandy looked at him surprised and then saw that he was looking straight past her. She whirled round and thought for an instant she was going to have a heart attack. Neville was standing right there in the doorway, wearing a pair of boxer shorts.

Mandy was rooted to the spot, unable even to figure out whose safety she was most worried about. Probably her own. If Neville got rid of Jimmy, she knew she'd be next in line for some serious licks. But, as for the words that would simply defuse the situation, she couldn't begin to think what they might be.

Then a small miracle occurred. Neville just said, 'Oh. All right, Jim?' like they were just saying hello in the street.

'Yeah, all right, Nev,' said Jimmy, and then, 'Paisley, eh, I'd have thought you were more of a polka-dot type.' Neville looked down at his boxers and laughed. Mandy sat down, bewildered, but not so bewildered that she didn't catch what happened next between Jimmy and Neville – a quick silent exchange that consisted of an inquisitive eyebrow-raise from Neville and a short affirmative nod from Jimmy.

Then Jimmy turned to her. 'Well,' he said, 'he come round to nick the kids again, has he? Take 'em back to St Lucia. Or was it Splott?' This time a little edge in the voice.

Mandy looked down at her hands, wondering how the hell she was expected to play this scene, feeling thoroughly rumbled. But then Jimmy laughed and said, 'Well, he is your husband, love.'

Then he switched tone and suddenly sounded businesslike. 'Listen,' he said, 'why don't you two put some clothes on and come back down, we've got some things to sort out.'

Mandy and Neville did as they were told, walked back upstairs, put some clothes on, didn't exchange a word. Mandy was furiously trying to make sense of the situation, trying to find her place in the web of guilt and misbehaviour. Any way she looked at it, she'd got to be in the wrong, but that didn't normally stop her apportioning blame elsewhere. Well, never explain never apologise, that was her motto, and as she walked back down the stairs she was feeling a little tingle of anticipation.

That's when Jimmy's mobile rang.

'All right,' said Jimmy, then, 'Shit,' then, 'Wait, just wait.' Then he clicked the phone off and didn't say anything at all for a few seconds.

'That was Mark,' he said eventually, and Mandy wondered who the hell he was talking about till she realised he wasn't talking to her at all but to Neville.

Neville didn't say anything, just waited for Jimmy to continue.

'Silly cunt's broken down up by St Mellons, like.'

'Serious?'

'Yeah, said the engine just cut out. Smoke coming out the front.'

Mandy switched off. She couldn't fucking believe it. She was just getting ready for a big fucking drama and, be honest, she was looking forward to it. Two blokes ready to go to war over her. But now she was written out of the damn script. Instead she was back watching a little play she'd seen too many times already. Seemed like she'd spent half her life sitting in kitchens with men who couldn't even manage to be proper villains. She knew what would happen next. The two of them would go out. Neville would borrow a van off someone – Wayne Ibadulla, probably – and then he'd go up to St Mellons and pick up whatever it was. Something electrical, most likely. God knows what Jimmy was going to do: ride shotgun in a fucking squad car for all she knew. Or cared. 'Cause suddenly she was sick of it. It wasn't Neville; she'd always known what he was like and she'd still gone for him, silly cow that she was. She'd even believed him when he gave her the old sob stuff about how there was nothing else out there for him 'cept a bit of thieving. But Jimmy, that was something else. Jimmy, he'd found something else, and now he was shitting on it.

'Get out,' she said.

They both turned and looked at her, and for a moment she couldn't tell them apart, the black guy and the white guy, so identical were their expressions, shocked but already figuring the odds.

'Both of you,' she said. And she wished she could keep and bottle whatever it was she had in her voice because there wasn't a peep. They got up and left like little lambs. And she knew it would be a while before either of them were back in her yard.

The Ship and Pilot

The way Col remembered it, the pirate radio station was mostly Ozzie's idea. OK, it was T-Bird who was the frontman, but it was Ozzie's idea in the first place, Col was sure. He'd first heard about it when he took his old lady down the community centre for some curry goat. She'd bought him a Dragon stout, but the sound of Harry calling the bingo numbers in the hall next door had been driving him mad, so he'd wandered off into the other room and found himself in the middle of some kind of meeting.

Mrs Harris and Leila from the school had been there. T-Bird had been sitting at the back sprawled across three seats keeping his eye on some little girl looked like she was from the paper. And Ozzie was near the front talking.

Now, Col's general reaction on seeing Ozzie was to duck out of the way. Ozzie had been his social worker back when Col was about fifteen, and they'd got on OK, but now Ozzie seemed to have some kind of mission to set Col on the straight and narrow. Either that or get him to join some protest or other.

But, before he could turn and leave, T-Bird spotted him, waved him over and grasped Col's hands in both of his like they were blood. Not that Col minded T-Bird – he was a mouthy fucker, but at least he had a bit of get up and go – it was just that he was a London geezer, been down here a couple of years, all right, but it still made a difference. Different rhythm down here.

Anyway, he was just leaning over to T-Bird, telling him he had to shoot, when Ozzie, still talking, turned round to survey his audience.

'Well,' said Ozzie, his ponytail flapping around behind him as he turned fully to face T-Bird and Col, 'good to see that this is an issue that gets the whole community interested.'

Cheeky bastard, thought Col, what did he mean by that? But he didn't say anything, not having a clue what the issue was. Didn't have to wait long to find out, though.

'So,' said Ozzie, 'you have some ideas for a community radio station then, Colin?'

'Nah, man, no,' said Col, 'I was just waiting to hear what you had to say, like.'

For his part, Ozzie was well pleased to see Col out there in the audience. Trouble with these kinds of initiatives, the ones aimed at the street-level guys, was that half the time the guys never knew you were taking the initiative in the first place.

Still, T-Bird had said he'd put the word out, get some of the brothers along, and it looked like this time the guy had delivered. Maybe it was to do with T-Bird being a Londoner like Ozzie, not that Ozzie had lived there in twenty years now, but he seemed to have a bit more ambition than a lot of the guys down here. Gave off a vibe as though things could happen.

So tonight, when Col asked him what his ideas were about the radio station, Ozzie got carried away and launched into a spiel that went beyond the usual multi-culti bullshit the councillors all wanted to hear. Instead he found himself making a speech that finally blossomed into a call for rebel radio – the true sound of the Cardiff Underground.

The moment he finished and turned round to look at the committee members, he knew he'd blown it. Renegade drum and bass was not what the council had been promised – more like gardening tips and the occasional Bob Marley record. Gardening tips! He couldn't believe some woman on the broadcasting sub-committee had actually said that to him. He wondered if the stupid cow had ever been to Butetown. Lot of use gardening tips are when you're living twelve floors up.

Of course the members didn't come right out and say it there and then. Ozzie got the usual polite round of applause when he finished talking, but he was sure he saw Don the local councillor roll his eyes at Mrs Harris, the so-called bloody community leader. And, sure enough, a moment later Mrs Harris was nodding to one of her cronies sat out in the audience, inviting her for her thoughts – which were the usual blather of well-meaning stuff about educating the kids and giving them a sense of pride. Ozzie wondered why she didn't just break into 'The Greatest Love of All' and have done with it.

Of course it all went down a storm and Mrs Ernestine Harris couldn't restrain herself from giving him a smirk, like you come down here telling black people what they want, well you don't know anything. What we want is gardening tips and self-improvement. Well, maybe she was right. Then he found himself looking at Col and nearly burst out laughing as he thought that there was a man could offer Butetown a few gardening tips. Col's hydroponic half hour.

The formal part of the meeting wound up pretty quickly after that, thank Christ, and Ozzie headed straight for the bar, elbowing the bingo-sated pensioners out of the way as he ordered up a pint of SA. He'd just taken the first gulp when he saw T-Bird and Col waving to him from the corner of the bar.

'That was great, man,' said T-Bird, putting his hand out and pulling Ozzie into a soul shake. 'Yeah, you had them jumping there, my man.'

Ozzie shook his head. 'No,' he said, 'I totally blew it. I should have just told them the bollocks they want to hear and got the station up and running.'

'You reckon?' said T-Bird.

'Yeah,' replied Ozzie. No way that bunch are interested in doing something radical.'

'So?' said T-Bird.

'So, what?' said Ozzie.

'So, what are you gonna do about it?'

Ozzie shrugged. 'Not much I can do, man. Just keep plugging away.'

'How about going pirate? That's what we need, a real rebel radio station. Innit, Col?'

Col, who was only half listening, nodded his head.

And that's how it started.

'Rainbow Radio,' said T-Bird. 'That's what we gotta call it.'

Ozzie and Col looked at each other and rolled their eyes; sounded exactly the sort of crap name Mrs Harris and her crew would have come up with. Still T-Bird chuntered on regardless.

'Soul and swing in the morning, bit of reggae round lunchtime, get things moving in the afternoon, garage and house, then get serious in the evenings. Time this city joined the 1990s, you know what I mean?'

Amens to that all round and a couple more drinks while they roughed out a programming schedule. Next morning, though, it seemed to Ozzie like one of those things you get excited about over a few beers but never do anything about.

So he was surprised a couple of days later, when opening his office post, to find a photocopied sheet inviting him to the first planning session for Rainbow Radio. ATTENDANCE BY INVITATION ONLY. The meeting was set for nine o'clock that night, the back bar in the Ship and Pilot.

And so that evening, after putting his daughter to bed and wolfing down a quick plate of tagliatelle, he was ready to go the minute his partner, Bethan, got in from her evening class. She laughed when he told her he was going down the docks to set up a pirate radio station, asked if he was sure the docks people really wanted to listen to Grateful Dead records. That was the trouble with living with someone fifteen years younger than you; they didn't always appreciate just what a long strange trip it had been. And didn't quite believe that a person could be forty-five years old and be able to get their head around speed garage as well as Garcia and Grisman.

Ozzie jumped on the bus on North Road, took it as far as the bus station, looked around for the docks bus, didn't see one and decided to start walking. It still gave him a buzz walking away from the town centre and under the bridge into Butetown. It was over twenty years ago now, but there was still a thrill attached to passing under a bridge you'd personally once blown up.

God knows, he wouldn't want to do another two years inside, but there still weren't many days went by without Ozzie missing that time, the early seventies, when you could talk about revolution and people didn't laugh at you. Now he was as keen as anyone to avoid all that 'those were the days – kids today are apathetic good-for-nothings who've never read a word of Trotsky' bullshit. But, still, it had been a time and he had been there. Not that running the youth centre wasn't worthwhile, serious, committed, blah, blah. But, anyway, the minute T-Bird had said the word 'pirate', well something in Ozzie's soul had stirred. And, hallelujah, there was a bus stopping right in front of him, saving him the long, windy walk up Bute Street.

It was five past nine when Ozzie arrived at the pub, and he wasn't entirely surprised to find himself the first one there. So he bought a drink and sat at the bar chatting to the barmaid, a cute little thing, name of Sarita, whose dad, it turned out, was one of the guys who'd run the Casablanca way back when, which reminded Ozzie just how old he was.

Around twenty past T-Bird turned up, cracking on about her indoors letting him off the leash. And, by half past, three more people had turned up. First of all Col. Ozzie still couldn't figure out Col, even though he had known him for nearly twenty years, for God's sake, since the days Col was a pissed-off kid and Ozzie had come out of prison and just started as a social worker – working for the man, way he used to look at it. The other two were women: a girl named Mandy, another one Ozzie had known since she was a kid, and who he'd seen DJing around the clubs, and with her was a dark, stocky girl with short locks. No one introduced her so he figured she was probably just Mandy's mate, brought along to have someone to chat to in the ladies.'

Ozzie ended up getting the drinks in, couple of K ciders for the girls, pint of Extra for T-Bird, orange juice for Col who was on some kind of martial-arts diet, least that's what he said.

Then they were all sat down and Ozzie was waiting for T-Bird or Col to get things going, seeing as it was one of them had called the meeting, but after a minute or two he figured that they were all waiting for him to start. So he did.

'Right,' he said, 'you've all heard about this community-radio thing that's being talked about? OK. Well, I know you two' – nodding at Col and T-Bird – 'realise that what's going on is a farce. A bunch of happy-clappy bollocks. So what T-Bird has suggested . . .'

Ozzie paused, aware that, although he had started talking to the group as a whole, he was now addressing Mandy almost exclusively. She had leaned in towards him the moment he started talking, while the others had leaned back. And when he'd said the word 'suggested', he could have sworn he'd seen her tongue dart out from between her small perfect teeth and run along her lips.

What was he thinking of? Quite apart from the fact he was committed elsewhere, the girl was young enough to be his daughter. Or was she? He did some rapid mental arithmetic: if he was forty-five and had met her fifteen years ago, when she was sixteen or so . . . Christ, that made her thirty. She probably had kids and stuff herself. It happened all the time: he'd seen kids grow up, have a family, screw up, have another family, all in the blink of an eye, while his own life drifted quietly along.

'So,' he returned to the plot, 'so T-Bird here has suggested we ignore all that local-government funding crap and set up our own station, a pirate station.'

'Yeah,' said everyone, more or less at once, and in the ensuing pause Ozzie realised that this wasn't going to be debated endlessly, it was a simple flat-out decision. All that remained was to get on with it.

'So, anybody know about the equipment side of things?'

'Yeah, man,' said T-Bird. 'Back up in the smoke I used to run with some brothers used to do a pirate thing.'

'So what do we need?'

'Well, turntables and a decent Mike, for starters.'

'We can use mine,' offered Mandy, and there was a chorus of approving grunts.

'What else?'

'Just a transmitter, really,' said T-Bird, 'plus a few leads and stuff you can pick up from Tandy's.'

'How about the transmitter?' asked Ozzie. 'Anyone know how much one of them costs?'

T-Bird shook his head, but then Col cut in. 'About four hundred and fifty to five hundred pounds, far as I knows. Bloke over Bristol might let us have one cheaper.'

'How much?'

'Well,' said Col, slightly embarrassed, 'I was thinking of doing a little bit of trade with the guy, you knows what I mean.'

'Well, great,' said Ozzie. 'Great. Thanks.'

'Yeah, but I'd still be out of pocket, like,' murmured Col.

'Oh, yeah, sure, about how much are we talking about then?' asked Ozzie.

''Bout a couple of hundred sounds right,' replied Col.

'I'll sort it.'

Ozzie glanced round in surprise. The black girl who'd come with Mandy had spoken. He looked at her closely for the first time. She was a small butch person. He couldn't quite decide whether he'd seen her before or not. The odd thing was the reaction her offer was getting. Col just stared at her, looking pissed off. T-Bird suddenly seemed preoccupied with what was going on on the pool table. Only Mandy looked enthusiastic, reaching over, squeezing the other girl's knee, saying, 'Nice one, Bobby.'

Then Ozzie got who she was: Bobby Ranger. Something of a legend in social services circles ever since she broke her social worker's arm when she was fifteen. That bastard Frank Evans had come into work, his arm in a sling. The whole place had nearly erupted in applause. If you'd ever seen the way he behaved with any teenage girl who looked all right, you'd know why. The creep never put in a complaint, transferred out to Carmarthen a couple of months later. Be ministering to the sheep now, they let him get close enough. That was Bobby Ranger. Ran with the City crew for a while back then too, he'd heard from some of the football boys he'd been working with.

'Just tell Maria how much, like,' Bobby added, speaking directly to Col. There followed a couple of seconds of really evil silence before Ozzie stepped in.

'Thanks for the offer, Bobby – it's Bobby, yeah? – but I can probably find the money in the centre's budget somewhere, if that'd help.'

A rapid series of nods indicated that it would indeed help. Bobby stood up, glowered at Col, and said she needed to go check on how her business was running, and that was more or less that.

The next couple of weeks, things moved along nicely. Col picked up the transmitter from Bristol. T-Bird produced a guy named Little Steve who actually understood how it all worked. Sitting in T-Bird's front room halfway up the Loudoun Square flats, he managed to connect the transmitter up to Mandy's turntables and Ozzie's old CD player for a quick trial blast.

Meanwhile the group met each Wednesday in the Ship and Pilot to plan things out and they decided to broadcast non-stop every weekend from Friday lunchtime to Sunday night.

Another fortnight, and the big day arrived. The transmitter was stuck on top of the flats, and the studio was set up in an empty flat a couple of floors from the top, which one of Col's brothers had the keys to. Word had been put round the community that 105.2 FM would be the place to be twelve noon on Saturday, and by half eleven, amazingly enough, there they all were. Ozzie, Col, T-Bird and Bobby. Mandy was due along later, around four, to take over from T-Bird.

It was around ten to that Ozzie said, innocently enough, 'Shouldn't we have some jingles?' and suddenly everyone realised they still didn't have a name for the station, let alone any jingles. T-Bird had been pushing for Rainbow Radio, which had drawn snorts of derision, but no one had come up with anything much better – Rebel Radio, Roots Radio, Bay FM, blah, blah. Around two minutes to twelve Bobby suddenly said TSOB – The Sound of Butetown – and everyone agreed just like that.

And then it was happening. T-Bird took the first shift. On the stroke of twelve he stuck McFadden and Whitehead's immortal 'Ain't No Stopping Us Now' on turntable one. At five minutes past twelve he said, 'Welcome to TSOB, your main man T-Bird here on the wheels of steel. That's the T-Bird in your area and, like the car, bra, I'm long, sleek and black.'

First time he said it, everyone in the studio cracked up. By four o'clock, though, when he'd said the same thing after every other bloody record, they were close to strangling him.

But, still, the bottles were being poured, the draw was making the rounds and there was a constant stream of visitors popping in to say they were picking the show up loud and clear.

At four there was something of a changing of the guard. A kid called Marcus came in to do a rap and swing session and he brought his own posse of teenagers with him. For Ozzie, at least, it was time to make a move.

Walking back home, he felt pleasantly out of it and well pleased with the way the station was shaping up. Next morning, however, he hurried to get to the studio at ten to present his own show – Back to the Old Skool with Count Ozzie', as he was billing it – and was a bit less than impressed to find the place deserted. According to the schedule they'd drawn up, someone called Mikey was supposed to have been presenting the Sunday morning champagne breakfast show. But, whoever this Mikey was, it didn't look like he'd made it out of bed.

Still, Ozzie pushed the faders up, stuck Elmore James's 'Dust My Broom' on the turntable and just enjoyed himself for the next four hours. He played everything from the blues to Salif Keita to a whole set of old-school hip-hop tunes. He played the funky Meters from New Orleans and segued them straight into the funky Red Beans and Rice from Cardiff. He played Billie Holiday and Dinah Washington and, in between records, he talked about the things that were on his mind. He read out bits from the Sunday papers, went on a bit about the bay development and the latest stupid plans. He was on the point of trying out a competition, just to see if there was anyone out there listening, when he realised that there wasn't a phone number anyone could ring. Have to get a mobile for the station, he decided.

The long and short of it was Ozzie was having the time of his life. He loved doing the radio, the time flew by and, when T-Bird showed up just before two, he felt oddly reluctant to hand over. Still, he stuck a Bill Withers tune on the deck, said goodbye and see you next week to the imaginary people at the other end of the microphone, and made space for T-Bird.

As he left the studio the last words he heard were, 'This is the T-Bird – like the car, bra, long, sleek and black – coming atcha with the sounds of the Prodigy, and a big shout out to all you good, good people down at Caesar's last night.'

Ozzie fled. If there was one thing he couldn't stand, it was the goddamn Prodigy. Back home, though, he was on a high. Bethan and a couple of mates were waiting for him and everyone loved the show and blah, blah, blah.

Over the next week, though, Ozzie's high turned to anxiety as he wondered whether anyone apart from the presenters' mates was listening to the station.

On Wednesday they had the usual meeting in the Ship, and Ozzie persuaded everyone that a mobile phone would be a good idea, which wasn't difficult once he said he'd be finding the money again.

Friday, though, T-Bird tried it out. He announced a competition on the air and gave out the phone number. Not a single person called.

So Ozzie was worrying a little as to whether the station would ever take off when, Friday night, his pub night, he went down the Oak. First person he saw was a six-foot-four old hippy with a great mane of long grey hair who everyone called the Colonel. The Colonel had his own personal spot at the corner of the bar, from which he propositioned every woman foolish enough to come within his orbit, but was held in a certain amount of respect as the pub's undisputed quiz-night king. As Ozzie approached the bar, the Colonel walked over, clapped him on the back and said, 'Brilliant show, butt, fucking brilliant.'

'Cheers,' said Ozzie, suddenly warming to the bloke. 'Thanks a lot. You all right for a drink?'

'Pint of Dark, butt, cheers. Tell you what would be good, though.'

'What?'

'Bit of racing.'

'You what?'

'Yeah, bit of racing news, a tip of the week, that kind of thing. People likes a flutter down the docks.'

Ozzie knew this was true.

'Colonel,' he said, 'you remember Andy I used to work with?'

The Colonel shook his head.

'Mr Serious, from up north. Most humourless Trot on the block.'

The Colonel shook his head again. 'Sorry, butt, got a memory for names but not faces. What too many mushrooms does for you.'

'Anyway,' said Ozzie, 'this guy Andy is out selling papers every Saturday morning, a rag called *Fight Racism, Fight Imperialism*. And he's doing the docks beat. Fair play to him, he's gone round every one of the flats there, all the way up to the stop of Loudoun Square. And most of the people who haven't threatened to set the dog on him have slammed the door in his face.

'And he's really thinking of jacking it in when, bingo, ninth floor, this sweet old lady, old Mrs Pinto, real old-school docks lady, never got over them knocking the old streets down, she opens the door, gives him a big smile. Andy says, "*Fight Racism, Fight Imperialism*, madam," and he can't believe she says, "All right, son, how much is it?" He's so overjoyed he just gives her it. She smiles again, wishes him all the best and God's blessing and all and, just as she shuts the door, she says, "Oh yes, I buys all the racing papers, me." '

The Colonel laughed. 'See what I mean? You got to go for it. You going to be on Sunday morning again?'

'No,' said Ozzie, 'I'm doing Saturday afternoons from now on.'

'Perfect,' said the Colonel. 'I'll bring along my tip of the day and give you a little bit of football chat too. Just tell us where to show up.' As if hypnotised, Ozzie complied, and with that the Colonel belched hugely and wandered off towards the music-room.

And so it came to pass that Saturday afternoon, quarter to three, just as Ozzie placed Curtis Mayfield's 'Pusherman' in the CD player, there was a clanking noise outside the studio door. Seconds later the Colonel entered, his long grey hair bound up in a ponytail, clutching a carrier bag full of bottles of Brains Dark in one hand, and a *Daily Mirror* and a copy of Bruce Springsteen's *Born to Run* in the other.

'All right, butt?' he said, and dragged a chair over close enough for Ozzie to savour the unmistakable smell of a man who's been in the pub since opening time.

'Got a mike for me then?'

Ozzie shook his head.

'Never mind, we'll just have to share. You introduce me and I'll shift over.'

Ozzie did as he was told. 'That was Curtis Mayfield,' he said, 'and any of you out there who haven't checked out the man's *New World Order* album should do so right now. One of the true greats. And now I've got a guest in the studio – he paused for a moment. Did the Colonel have a real name? Christ knows. Christ knew why they called him the Colonel, come to that – 'come to talk about today's sport and racing. Here's the Colonel.'

There was a distinct pause and several heavy clunks were to be heard as Ozzie shifted out of his chair and the Colonel moved in, and after a long pause the old hippy bent his frame down to the mike and started talking.

'How you doing, boys and girls? Anyone out there want to get rich this afternoon? Well, stay tuned for the Colonel's Saturday Best. I'll tell you now, it's running in the four o'clock at Doncaster, but you'll have to listen to me slagging off the City for a while before I'll tell you its name, and before that you'll have to listen to a few words from God.' At which point listeners were confronted with another lengthy pause as the Colonel unpacked his Bruce Springsteen album and handed it to Ozzie with instructions to play track one, side one. 'Thunder Road'.

Ozzie was dying inside. He couldn't believe he'd let this idiot rock fan come in and ruin his show. No one round here was tuning in to listen to Bruce the Boss Springsteen.

Things went from bad to worse when, after the song finally finished, the Colonel launched into what seemed to Ozzie to be a completely incomprehensible rant about the failings of

Cardiff City and its players, management, chairman, caterers, even the poor bloody car-parking attendants.

At the end of the rant, the Colonel reached over before a stunned Ozzie could stop him, and plonked the needle down so hard it bounced a couple of times before settling down to play another bloody Bruce Springsteen track. As the tune started playing, Ozzie turned the microphone off and said, in a tone that barely stopped short of hostility, that that was enough.

'Hey,' said the Colonel, 'what about my racing tip?'

'OK, give them the racing tip, and then hand back to me.' He took a deep breath. The Colonel was a big bloke, and there was no point in antagonising him. 'You've done a great job.'

'Yeah?' said the Colonel, pleased. 'It's a good laugh, butt. Tell you what, why don't I ask if anyone wants to phone in, have a chat about what I was saying.'

'Fine,' said Ozzie, figuring that the ensuing silence should deflate the Colonel efficiently enough.

So, as the anthemic strains of 'Born to Run' faded away, the Colonel stuck the faders up, announced that today's finger-lickin'-good selection from the Colonel was Mahatma Coat in the four o'clock at Doncaster – 'Put your shirt on it' – and then handed back to Ozzie with the words, 'Take it easy, but make sure you take it.'

Ozzie thanked the Colonel, cursing himself for sounding like Smashy and Nicey as he did so, and then gave out the phone number, 'for anyone interested in having a chat with the Colonel about sporting matters'. And he was frankly astonished when, fifteen seconds later, just as the intro to the next record started, the phone rang.

The Ship and Pilot

It was a bloke wanting to argue the toss about the City manager. Ozzie had no choice but to stick the mike back up and pass him over to the Colonel. And, while they seemed to be talking a foreign language to Ozzie, who had a pretty thoroughgoing contempt for all forms of sport, the Colonel was clearly handling it like a pro.

After that the phone rang two or three more times. It was remarkable. To be honest, Ozzie had always found the Colonel a borderline-annoying drunk and drink cadger, and now he turned out to be a fast, witty conversationalist. More than that, it had to be said the Colonel's full-on Cardiff accent gave him a natural advantage as a local broadcaster over Ozzie's flattened-out middle-class vowels.

Wednesday night, TSOB's founding crew had their regular get-together in the Ship and Pilot, chance to discuss how things were going. T-Bird arrived just at the same time as Ozzie.

'Great show on Saturday, man,' he said as Ozzie was getting the drinks in. ''Specially your mate the Colonel.'

'Oh,' said Ozzie, who'd been expecting to get a bit of a hard time for letting some bloke come in and play Springsteen records. 'Didn't figure you were much of a Bruce fan.'

'No,' said T-Bird, looking at him blankly, 'I was talking about his Saturday tip, Mahatma Coat. Fourteen to one, man. I was sitting at home, right, chilling, listening to your show, and then this geezer comes on. Mate of yours, so I figure he knows what he's talking about, and I thought fuck it and went round the bookie's. Fiver on the nose, seventy quid, mate.'

Col turned up ten minutes later and went through the same routine more or less word for word. Except he'd stuck a tenner on, which struck Ozzie as a rather excessive gesture of faith in the Colonel but had clearly paid off handsomely. Then Bobby showed up and said how much she liked the bloke who'd given the City some stick, and Ozzie started to feel half like a proud parent and half pissed off that nobody had anything to say about the rest of his show.

Next week it was even worse. Saturday, the calls had started practically as soon as the Colonel showed up, a copy of *The River* with him this time. Apparently the listeners kept on phoning till halfway through Mandy's swing and rap show that evening, pissing her off considerably, as sport was not one of her big interests. By then the Colonel's tip, a ten-to-one shot called Nova Express, had steamed in at Wincanton, and it sounded like half Butetown had got in on the bet.

Come the following Wednesday, Ozzie had had a call from T-Bird suggesting he bring along 'my man the Colonel' to the Ship, so the rest of the crew could have a little chat with the geezer, y'know what I mean.

Ozzie certainly did know what he meant when he and the Colonel showed up at nine to find Col and T-Bird already sitting at the bar, a copy of the *Sporting Life* sitting on the bar in between them.

T-Bird had the Colonel's hand clasped in a soul shake before he could get his coat off, and Col had him a pint of Guinness in record time.

'So, big man,' said T-Bird as they sat down in the corner table, 'you getting rich then?'

The Colonel shook his head. 'No, butt, I spent too long making the bookies rich. I just make the tips these days.'

T-Bird laughed. 'Your loss, man. You got a gift for it, far as I can see.'

'Nah,' said the Colonel, 'just on a little bit of a roll. Got to stop soon.'

'Yeah, well,' said T-Bird and then, doing his best to sound casual but failing horribly, 'so, you got any ideas about tomorrow's races, then? Me and Col were just looking over the form a little . . .'

'Yeah,' said the Colonel. 'Go for a Yankee. Miles of Aisles in the two fifteen at Ripon. Hey Jude in the three o'clock at Doncaster and Interzone in the four fifteen back at Ripon.'

'Yeah,' said T-Bird, whipping out a pen, 'could you give us that again?'

'I could,' said the Colonel, 'but I won't 'cause it was bollocks. One tip a week. Saturday afternoon, that's all I can manage.' He stopped and held his head between his hands. 'I got to ration the power.'

T-Bird laughed, aiming for friendly but coming off as mildly irritated. 'I hear you, man. Saturday's fine.'

Ozzie was racking his brains for something to change the subject to. He could see that the Colonel was getting a little annoyed at being taken for a freak show. And seeing as he was a) the station's golden goose and b) a seriously big bloke, it would be best all round if he was calmed down. But before Ozzie could say anything, Mandy chipped in.

'Why'd they call you the Colonel?'

It was an obvious question, and one Ozzie himself didn't know the answer to, so he leaned forward to hear the big man's answer. But the Colonel shrugged and said, 'Just a nickname the guys gave me years ago.'

Then Bobby jumped in. 'Fucking hell,' she said, 'I knows who you are. You used to play for the City, is it?'

The Colonel shook his head, but there was a half smile round his mouth.

'Yeah,' she went on, 'I remember you, you were like the first sweeper the City ever had back when I was a kid. Ronnie something, isn't it?'

The Colonel put his hand up. 'Yeah. OK, OK. Less of the Ronnie, please.'

'You were great,' said Bobby and turned to address the others. 'He was brilliant. It was like having Franz bloody Beckenbauer in the team. That's why they called you the Colonel, 'cause they used to call him the General.'

The Colonel looked embarrassed. 'Yeah, well, maybe, love. Anyway, you can't hardly have been old enough . . .'

'Nah,' she said. 'Older than I look, me. I must have been nine or ten I saw you playing. And I've got some videos . . .' She tailed off, realising that everyone was staring at her now. 'Yeah, well, bit of an anorak me, you know what I mean? Anyway, what happened? You only played a couple of years. Seventy five, six – around then, wasn't it?'

The Colonel laughed. 'Bit of a problem with the old recreational substances. I was teaching a few of the boys how to relax before a game, like, and the manager, miserable Scots git always chopsing on about getting my hair cut, walked in the boot-room and, bang, I was fucking out of there. Joke of it was our left wing used to have four pints in the pub before he went out to play. Couldn't see where the touchline was half the time, manager never said a dicky bird. I could have gone somewhere else, I suppose, but, be honest, I was never that bothered about playing professional.'

'So what d'you do then, mate?' asked T-Bird.

'Went to work for my brother-in-law, on the cars, like. Respray work and stuff.'

'Didn't you play any more football?'

'Played one game for my mate's works team. Halfway through the first half, bloke clattered me, broke my leg. I thought, fuck that for a game of soldiers. Last time I touched a ball, apart from in the park with my kids, like.'

'So you don't fancy turning out for a little team we got down here then, mate?'

'Christ, T-Bird, leave the man alone,' said Col.

'Yeah,' chipped in Bobby, 'leave the man alone. He wants to play football, he'll play it, won't he?'

T-Bird put his hands up. 'Hey, no offence,' he said, and then, 'What was that music you were playing last week? The last thing you played before the tip?'

Ozzie almost sighed out loud with relief. The Colonel had shown signs of beginning to get pissed off. And, though he'd never seen it for himself, he'd heard stories about what happened when the Colonel lost his temper. This was six foot three and fifteen stone of hippy you didn't want to enrage.

The rest of the evening passed off amiably enough. Next Saturday, the Colonel showed up right on cue with a copy of *Lucky Town* – 'the most underrated album the Boss ever made' – and a hot tip. The hot tip – a nag called Dead Fingers Talk running in the four o'clock at Catterick – duly strolled home at twelve to one.

At least it was twelve to one every place in the British Isles except Butetown. Way Col told it to Ozzie later, what happened was a sight to see. Two o'clock, there's a whole bloody line-up of people queuing up outside the bookie's.

No one's inside watching the racing on TV, everyone's outside, transistor radios clutched to their heads waiting for the Colonel's tip. And it's not just the usual bookie's crowd either: the old geezers in their pork-pie hats. Today there's grandmothers in their Sunday go-to-church dresses, and mums with pushchairs, and they're all asking how to fill the forms in, and all it needed was a bloody hot-dog van to make a street party of it, with Bruce Springsteen providing the soundtrack.

'Course it was obvious, really, what was going to happen next. First four people in, making the same bet on a horse the bookie's never even heard of. It puts the wind up him, 'specially when he sees the queue coming through the door. He calls head office. The odds go down to six to one, and then down to two to one. And after a few minutes, they have to call the police because it looks like there's going to be a riot out there, people screaming about how they were told it was twelve to one.

Not that Col saw that bit because, the second him and T-Bird clocked the queue, they'd run over to Col's motor and hammered it over City Road way, found a nice empty bookie's and put their money down there.

Still, Col's brother Roy had been down the bookie's in Butetown, and he said it had been touch and go for a moment. But the police showed up before anyone could trash the bookie's like they were threatening to, and then, when it got to about half three, a lot of the boys decided to try and find another bookie's as well. No use arguing the toss after the race was run.

By the next week, though, things were crazy. Col was arranging to call his cousin up in Birmingham to put some money on there. T-Bird had the same kind of deal with his mum back up London.

'Don't you worry he might pick a loser?' Ozzie asked Col at the Wednesday-night meeting.

'Hasn't yet, has he?' chipped in T-Bird before Col could answer.

'Yeah, but, Christ, it's just a lucky streak – three out of three. All the more likely it's going to come to an end next time.'

Col looked at T-Bird. T-Bird looked at Col, who spoke up. 'You've got to be a gambler to feel it, boss. Sometimes you just knows things are going your way. You don't know why but you don't question it. The man's on a roll.'

'Yeah,' said T-Bird. 'Where is he, by the way?'

Ten minutes later the question was answered. The Colonel walked into the pub looking like Daddy Cool. Well, the Colonel looked like he always did. Tight jeans, big old leather jacket, long frizzy grey hair. What made him look like Daddy Cool were the women hanging off each of his arms. On his left was a girl named Stephanie, worked in Black Caesar's and was one seriously fit individual. As was the girl on his right arm, Bernice.

'Fucking hell,' said T-Bird reverently.

'Man's on a roll, all right,' said Col.

Saturday afternoon, the studio was a zoo. The Colonel showed up with a half-empty bottle of brandy in one hand, a bumper-sized spliff in the other, and a full-scale posse in attendance. Four or five girls plus a couple of Ibadulla cousins plus a couple of old guys from the Oak: a boxing trainer name of Bernie and an old middleweight used to be a big deal in the fifties, Charlie something. Every single person there seemed to be carrying a mobile.

Ozzie was finding it almost impossible to think. He'd lined up a terrific little segment. Working back and back from Mase to Bootsy's Rubber Band to James Brown and then spinning off via Miles's *Bitches Brew* to a couple of cuts from the Sun Ra singles set. The secret history of the funk with Count Ozzie, he was billing it as, but delivering it in the midst of half a dozen people shouting at each other and down their phones was no fun at all.

Then it was time for the Colonel. Ozzie was half expecting him to show up this time with Shabba's *Trailer Load of Girls* and have done with it. But no, the attention had clearly not driven the Boss from his place next to the Colonel's heart. He plonked himself down on the seat next to Ozzie, who moved over to allow him to put a copy of *Darkness at the Edge of Town* on the turntable, and stuck on the desperately mournful 'Racing in the Street'.

Ozzie looked at the Colonel. All of a sudden, he could see the man looked tired, going on exhausted.

'Christ, man,' said the Colonel, dragging heavily on the spliff before passing it to Ozzie, 'I'm getting too old for this shit.'

Ozzie shook his head, smiling, the smile starting to disappear as he smelt something acrid behind him. He turned to see one of the Ibadulla boys firing up a rock. Ozzie spun round in his chair, said, 'Oi, mate, what do you think you're doing? This is a pirate radio station. Chances are the police are sussing out where we are right now. 'Specially as half the bloody world's already here. Look, the police show up, not only will they haul off all our equipment, but they'll bust you and most probably me and the Colonel as well. So leave it out, right.'

Even as the words were coming out of his mouth, he

couldn't believe he was saying them. Veteran anarchist like himself telling people not to take drugs 'cause the police might bust them. Still, there was something about the dumb bloody arrogance of the way the kid was carrying on in what – he couldn't help it – felt like his studio that had enraged him.

The guy stood up, also clearly unable to believe that some social-worker twat would get in his face about a little rock, and the situation was well on the way to bad news when the record stopped.

The Colonel said, 'Afternoon, everyone, that was the Boss with the greatest of all his car songs, you take my word for it. I'm the Colonel and I'm not going to hang about this afternoon, my top tip is running in just half an hour's time in the two thirty at Exeter, and it's a fifteen-to-one shot – a filly name of Yage, that's Y-A-G-E, Yage.'

Suddenly all thoughts of violence disappeared as everyone except Ozzie and the Colonel reached for their mobile phones.

Ozzie decided that discretion was the better part of valour and took the chance to gather up his records and head out the door. As he left he clapped the Colonel on the shoulder and the old hippy turned round, waved and mouthed the words, 'Sorry, man,' just as he raised the faders on 'Badlands'. At the time Ozzie thought he was talking about the chaos in the studio.

The horse won, of course. Ozzie heard about it in the Old Arcade. He stopped off there for a pint on his way home, try and take the edge off his mood before he returned to his family. Seemed like half the pub had had money on Yage, but no one had managed to get fifteen to one. The bookies had her down to evens by the time the race started. And they'd still put money on. Ozzie could scarcely credit it. Who did they think the Colonel was?

It was at the Wednesday meeting that Ozzie suspected something was up. T-Bird didn't show and neither did the Colonel. Even then, Ozzie wouldn't have made much of it if Col hadn't been so uncharacteristically agitated.

'Something's going on, boss,' he said. 'Bobby saw T-Bird coming out the community centre with Ernestine, didn't you, Bob?'

Bobby nodded. Ozzie was more bewildered by the fact that Bobby and Col were speaking to each other than anything else. T-Bird had explained the tension between them, the little matter of Col's baby mother Maria being with Bobby.

'You got to ask some questions, boss,' said Bobby, her big brown eyes focused firmly on Ozzie. 'Ask them council people what's going on.'

'Yeah,' said Col and Mandy in chorus, and Ozzie realised that what was motivating them all was a real concern for the station.

'OK,' said Ozzie, 'no problem. I'll have a few words. But I shouldn't worry too much. The council never decided anything in less than a decade.'

'Thanks, boss,' said Col, 'and if you've got a chance, like, why don't you go see your man, the Colonel. Fucking T-Bird we can live without, but we needs the Colonel.'

Ozzie nodded again. 'Do what I can.'

So, Friday night, Ozzie went up the Oak, as per usual. He wasn't sure if the Colonel would be there or not. And if he was there he was half expecting him to come complete with entourage.

As it turned out, though, the Colonel was there, all right. But he wasn't at his usual perch on the bar. Instead he was sitting alone at a table in the corner with a great pile of newspapers and form guides in front of him. On seeing Ozzie, though, he realised an arm and waved him over.

'Ozzie, man,' he said, 'I've lost it.'

'Lost what?'

'The knack, mate, the gift.'

Ozzie just stared at him, still not quite sure what he was talking about.

'My Saturday tip, man, I haven't got a clue what it's going to be.'

'Oh,' said Ozzie, 'isn't that what you've got all this stuff for?' waving at the pile of papers.

'No,' said the Colonel, 'you don't get it. The last few weeks I've just known. I've looked at the day's racing and something's just jumped out at me. Don't ask me why, but I've just known those horses were going to do it. This week – nothing.'

'Yeah, well, don't worry. You've had an incredible run. People have got to understand you can't be right every time.'

The Colonel shook his head. ' 'Course that's what they should think, but they don't. They think four out of four the Colonel's the magic man. Tomorrow half Cardiff's going to go and bet on whatever sodding horse I say. And, when it limps in bloody fifth, they're all going to want to kill me. What am I going to do, Oz?'

'Just don't give them a tip, then. Tell 'em you just don't know.'

'No good. They'll think I'm just keeping it to myself or

giving it to some syndicate. People'll probably storm the bloody station. It's madness out there, Oz, madness.'

Oz rolled his eyes, did the only helpful thing he could think of, which was to supply the Colonel with another pint of Dark, and then left the big man to his fevered studies.

Just as he was leaving, though, he stopped by the Colonel's table again and said, 'I could always tell them you're sick, man, if you don't want to come in.'

'No,' said the Colonel, 'I'll be there.'

And so he was. In fact he turned up about an hour earlier than usual, just about a half hour into Ozzie's show. Ozzie was doing a little subliminal broadcasting, segueing Barbara Lynn's 'You'll Lose a Good Thing' into Doris Duke's 'I'm a Loser' into Harold Melvin's 'The Love I Lost'.

The Colonel was on his own again. And not so much as a can of lager on his person, just a copy of Springsteen's *Nebraska*, the mournful acoustic one, in a carrier bag.

He just sat there for a while, listening to Ozzie play records and chat about this and that, but hardly saying a word. Finally, around half one, he leaned over to Ozzie, handed him the album and said, 'Tell you what, Oz, d'you mind playing all of side one?'

Ozzie gulped, then shrugged. On TSOB the Colonel got what the Colonel wanted. A couple of times, as the record played, he tried to engage the Colonel in conversation, but he just shook his head, wrapped in contemplation of the music, far as Ozzie could tell.

The last track on the side had just started, and Ozzie was wondering what the Colonel was going to do next, as he hardly seemed in the mood to talk about football, when all hell broke loose.

From the outer room there was the unmistakable sound of sledgehammer hitting door. Ozzie, moving quickly, with a rush of adrenalin that took him back to the old days, just had time to grab his own record boxes and stick them in a cupboard, then stick up the fader and shout, 'We'll be going off air in a moment, the studio's being raided,' before the room was full of police.

They were there for about an hour. Dismantling equipment and bundling it up, in between while taking the chance to have a bloody good sniff around for any sign of drugs. Thankfully there was nothing around. Even the Colonel seemed to have showed up clean. So, after a bit of huffing and puffing, and once they realised that Ozzie was a vaguely respectable member of society, they decided not to bother taking them down the station, just took names and addresses and told them to piss off.

Walking down the stairs, the Colonel laughed for the first time that day. 'Tell you what, Oz,' he said, 'every single fucking one of those coppers must have asked me what my tip of the day was.'

'So, d'you tell them?'

'Oh yes, I told them, all right. Gave 'em some three-legged nag running at Aintree, be a miracle if it even finishes the damn race.' And he laughed again.

Outside the flats, they ran into a welcoming committee: Col, Bobby and Mandy. All of them looking madder than hell.

Mandy spoke first. 'T-Bird,' she said.

'What?' said Ozzie.

'He was there,' said Mandy. 'I came over second I heard you on the radio. Two minutes I must have been there. Police tried to stop me, told them I was visiting my nan up the top. And he was there, outside the flat. Tried to keep out of sight, but I clocked him. The big yellow streak of piss was trying to hide by the lift but I clocked him. Bastard must have showed them where to go.'

'Oh well,' said Ozzie, with a sidelong glance at the Colonel, 'least the bookies will be happy.'

No one managed a laugh. Instead they all headed round the Ship for a drink. Which was a bad idea too. People kept coming by their table to say how great the station was, and they didn't just happen to know today's tip, did they? Even Kenny Ibadulla came over to have a word. When he heard what had happened, he offered to hold a fundraiser in the club, pay for some new gear. But really it felt to Ozzie like all they were doing was huffing and puffing.

Back on the street that afternoon, it was almost comical. Ozzie and the Colonel walked back together through town and everywhere they went there were people fiddling with their radios, trying to tune into TSOB. Then, just as they were heading for home, he picked up a copy of the *Echo*. And there it was, page three. A story about the police busting the radio station. A couple of paras of the usual party-line police bullshit, a ho-ho para about the Colonel and the bookies would be celebrating tonight. And then this:

Plans are afoot to launch a brand-new community station for the Cardiff Docks. To be known as Rainbow Radio, the service is scheduled to go on air in just two weeks' time, according to Community Radio Trust chair Ernestine Harris. Rainbow Radio's managing director will be the well-known local DJ, Darrell 'T-Bird'

Simpson. One question remains – will the Colonel, scourge of the Cardiff bookies, return to the airwaves?

Ozzie looked at the Colonel. 'How the hell did they know that? The raid only happened a couple of hours ago and the story's there already. Fucker must have told them it was happening.'

He waited for the Colonel to join in slagging off the long, sleek and black one. But instead he saw the Colonel's face contract into an expression of pure misery.

'Christ,' he said then, 'it was you too, Colonel. You were in on it, weren't you?'

Slowly, the Colonel nodded. 'I couldn't do it, Oz, I couldn't let everyone down, like. I was just going to say there was no tip today. Then I got a call from T-Bird, like, sounding me out, whether I wanted to join his station. So I says yes, thinking I'd find out what was going on. And he gives me the spiel – all be just the same 'cept I'll be getting paid for it. And then he says it might be an idea not to show up at the station today.'

Ozzie shook his head, puzzled. 'Then what's the problem, Colonel, you weren't in with him, were you?'

'No, but I should have said something – maybe we could have moved the gear. Truth is, I wanted them bastards to come in, save me screwing up on my tip. My fault, boss.'

The two of them stayed silent for a little while, walking back past the prison now and on into Adamsdown.

'One thing, though,' said the Colonel.

'What?'

'T-Bird was bugging me for my tip of the day. Said they'd

given him some upfront development money and he was planning on investing it. So I gave him the tip, all right.'

Ozzie started laughing. 'Came last, yeah?'

The Colonel started laughing too. 'No, mate,' he said, 'what d'you take me for? It won, didn't it.'

And that was the last anyone saw of T-Bird.

The Glastonbury Arms

After the radio station was closed down, Col and Ozzie used to meet up from time to time for a drink. At first it was mostly just to run down T-Bird, speculate on how much money he got away with and to wonder why on earth anyone would have trusted a guy like that, a line of thought that tended to peter out when they realised that they'd both trusted the guy.

Then they would meet for the ostensible purpose of Col supplying some grade-A hydroponic homegrown for Ozzie's domestic consumption. But basically what it was was that, after twenty years of knowing each other, since Col had been a bad boy and Ozzie a trainee social worker, they'd finally found it easy enough to be in one another's company. So they would meet up, sometimes in the Ship and sometimes right on the edge of town in the Glastonbury, which used, Col remembered, to be full of hippies and bikers but had lately been done up in order to attract the suit-and-tie brigade.

And it was in here one night that Col finally got round to asking Ozzie the question he'd always wanted to ask.

'Ozzie,' he said, 'did you really blow up the Butetown bridge back in the seventies?'

Ozzie laughed, put his hands up in surrender. 'Yes, your honour, but I'm a reformed character now. 'Course I did, don't you remember?'

'No,' said Col. 'Well, I remember something happening

about the bridge but I was just a kid. Didn't pay no attention. What happened?'

'It's a long story.'

'There's no hurry on, man, far as I can see. Take your time.'

'All right, then,' said Ozzie, and he got up and got a couple more pints in before settling down in his seat and saying, 'OK, first thing you should know, I was a member of a group called – don't laugh – the White Panthers. It was a group started by some guy in Detroit as, like, a white support group for the Black Panthers. Anyway, there were a bunch of us in Cardiff, we were well into it. You've got to remember this was the early seventies, the Angry Brigade were blowing stuff up, the IRA were blowing stuff up. Basically, you wanted to be taken seriously, you had to blow something up.'

A Saturday morning in the summer of 1976, Ozzie left the dynamite at home while he went out to get the paper. He would have been back in five minutes easy if he hadn't stopped to look in the guitar-shop window. There was a Fender Jaguar bass in there, and he knew it was hardly a revolutionary priority, but he coveted it. Trying to sound like the MC5 with a tinny little piece of shit bass like he had at the moment wasn't easy.

Anyway, he was only looking, but it was while he was standing there that old T-Bone came up to him.

'All right, mi brethren,' said T-Bone, and Ozzie couldn't help but be pleased. He knew that T-Bone was putting him on, but still it was a slight worry for Ozzie and the rest of the Cardiff chapter of the White Panthers that they sometimes seemed a little, well, isolated from the local black people.

'So, I check you at the funeral this afternoon. Rastaman?'

Ozzie had not quite come to grips with this Rasta business. The last year or two, it seemed to have caught on. Some kind of religious thing. Far as he could see, T-Bone calling him Rastaman was just taking the piss because he had long hair. So he grinned and nodded and bent his long skinny frame down towards the stocky T-Bone and asked, 'What funeral?'

T-Bone stood back in an attitude of exaggerated shock. 'Mi brethren, mi good, good brethren, Louis Hammer. He died last Monday.'

'Oh shit, man,' said Ozzie. He knew who the Hammer was, of course. Anyone who was out and about on the Cardiff pub scene did. The Hammer was this blind blues guy. He'd always be wearing a suit and a hat and dark glasses, played a big old semi-acoustic, would just set up in the corner of a pub and start playing. Wasn't exactly Ozzie's cup of tea, to be honest. When it came down to it, Ozzie pretty much thought the Cream had got the blues down. There was something a bit too countrified about the Hammer. But, still, he was the real thing.

'Shit,' he said again. 'The Hammer was the real thing, man.'

T-Bone nodded, said, 'Yes indeed. And we're going to send the brother off, big time, down the bay. Be a marching band, the whole deal. Start outside the Casablanca, two o'clock. So, I check you later?'

Ozzie nodded, said, 'Sure,' already wondering what that was going to do to their plan. Christ, it could be perfect. 'Later,' he said then, wondering whether T-Bone was going to engage him in one of those complicated handshake rituals. But T-Bone just touched his tam and said, 'Later, man. Seen.'

Ozzie stood still for a moment, pondering. Then he headed back past the post office to the phone box.

Half an hour later, and he was round at Terry's place over in Grangetown, smoking a joint. It kind of went without saying that if you were round at Terry's you would be smoking a joint. Terry wasn't even dressed yet. He was just sitting there on the edge of the bed, his black hair, normally puffed up into an Afro, collapsed on one side from sleep, his skinny white hands shaking slightly as he skinned up. His lady was in the kitchen making some breakfast for them all.

'A funeral procession. Man, that's perfect,' Terry said after a while. 'We wait till it's coming down Bute Street and then we go for it.'

'Yeah,' said Ozzie, 'great.' And then he paused for a moment. 'Only thing was, I thought it would be good if we went to the funeral. Put in a presence, y'know what I mean. It's going to be a big day for the black community and, y'know, there's a lot of people don't know about what we're doing.'

Terry didn't say anything, just toked deeply on the joint a couple of times, then he shouted through to the kitchen that he was starving and took a couple more tokes.

'You're right. Let's get all the cadres out on the streets for the funeral. Full dress. Then it's up to one of us from the operational cell to do the other thing. And then they'll know about us, all right.'

The operational cell was comprised of precisely two people: Ozzie and Terry. The thing that they were planning to do, the thing that was going to launch the Cardiff chapter of the White Panthers into the big time, was that they were going to blow up the Bute Street bridge, cutting off the railway line from London to Cardiff and commemorating the first British race riots, which happened in Cardiff back in 1919, fifty-seven years ago that day.

'All right,' said Ozzie, 'which one of us is going to do the thing?'

They were very careful, Ozzie and Terry, not to come right out and say what the thing was. It was an article of faith that the state was listening to your every word.

'Toss a coin,' said Ozzie facetiously.

'May as well,' said Terry, after a moment, and so they did.

Ozzie called tails and he was wrong. Terry looked pensive, and then said, 'Great, well, I'll take care of the business. You go round up the cadres and we'll meet at your place around one. You've got the, uh, provisions, ready?'

Ozzie nodded and Terry said, 'Cool,' and he genuinely seemed relaxed about the whole thing. Ozzie, on the other hand, was feeling so tense that, despite the dope, he couldn't sit still. 'Right,' he said, 'I'll get moving,' and with that he stood up and headed for the door. As he left, he could see Terry getting up and walking into the kitchen in search of his fried egg, joint swinging in his left hand.

Outside, Ozzie took a couple of deep breaths and decided which of the cadres to round up first. It didn't take long. Gwyneth was easily the most appealing option. For starters, she would be awake by now and, further to that, Ozzie's crush on her was getting to the point where even he realised it was resembling dog-like devotion and that, if he didn't do something about it soon, it was going to get pitiful. Today was a big day already, may as well go for it.

That, at least, was the plan. And, as Ozzie walked round to the house in Roath where Gwyneth lived with a couple of other members of the Women's Action Group, he could feel the rightness of it swelling in his chest. Found himself making crap jokes to himself along the lines of two big bangs on the same day.

Got to the front door, rang on the bell and one of the kids, a little boy, opened up. Ozzie said hello and walked upstairs to Gwyneth's room. As he approached the door, he heard a groan, but he kept going and knocked on the door and was just about to open it when he heard a strained female voice shout, 'Go away,' and then a man laugh and then the unmistakable sounds of a man and a woman doing the thing they do.

Abashed, not to say thoroughly pissed off, Ozzie retreated downstairs to the kitchen. A woman called Lilac was there chopping up vegetables on the big wooden table. The kettle was on so Ozzie accepted a cup of tea and then he spent the next fifteen minutes being quizzed about football teams by the little boy who, Ozzie supposed, must have been a bit starved of male company, living in this house with three women and his little sister. Though there was a man there at the moment, all right.

A little while later he found out who the man was. Gwyneth came downstairs first, long dirty-blonde hair piled up on top of her head, wearing some kind of loose-fitting ethnic dress, with, as far as Ozzie could tell, and he was doing his best, nothing underneath it. She put the kettle back on, said hello and, 'Oh, when did you come round? I didn't hear you,' to Ozzie, who prevented himself from grinding his teeth. An act of self-denial he had to repeat a minute or so later when Gwyneth's bloke came downstairs and proved to be none other than Red Mike, another White Panther cadre.

'Fookin' 'ell,' said Red Mike, as was his wont, 'look what the cat dragged in.'

Ozzie somehow raised a smile and then looked at Gwyneth and said, 'D'you think we could have a word?' nodding his head towards the door.

'Yeah, OK, sure,' said Gwyneth, and she led the way to the front room, Ozzie and Red Mike behind. Red Mike was rolling his eyes towards Gwyneth, and then doing everything but raising his fist and going 'Phwhorrrr!' but Ozzie affected not to notice.

In the front room, which was freezing even on a summer's day like this, Ozzie did his best to take charge of the situation. Told the other two about the funeral and that they needed to meet up at his at one. 'Shit,' he said, looking at his watch, 'it's half eleven now.'

Gwyneth said she would fetch Rose and bring her round. Red Mike reckoned he could get hold of Ken and Dafydd. 'Be in the pub by now, I know those two daft bastards,' he said. Ozzie said that would be great, he had a couple of things to get together. And then, he couldn't resist adding, there might be a bit of a surprise later on; just to remind the others that he was an operational cadre and worthy of respect.

Shit, he said to himself as he waited at the bus stop outside Gwyneth's. Red Mike, how could she go for that carrot-topped northern twat?

Walking back up Neville Street, he was faintly relieved to see it was still there. The flat was in one of two buildings that had been built to fill in one of Hitler's little holes, and Ozzie was a tad nervous that having a dozen sticks of gelignite stuck in his fridge might lead to a kind of repeat performance.

Still, it was hard to believe it was really going to happen. The White Panthers' Cardiff chapter was finally going to put itself on the world map.

Back in the flat, he gingerly checked the fridge, then headed into the front room where he stuck a Traffic album on the record player and sat down to check through the instructions in *The Anarchists' Cookbook* one more time.

Over the next half hour the rest of the chapter showed up, Gwyneth and Rose first. Before Rose – small and dark in some kind of gypsy outfit – could finish rolling up or Ozzie could make the tea, Terry was there wearing his greatcoat over jeans and a T-shirt, carrying the constituent parts of the group's banner.

'All right, girls,' he said as came into the front room, 'you two mind putting this together,' depositing the banner on the floor. 'Ozzie and me just got a couple of things to talk over.'

So Terry and Ozzie went into the bedroom. Terry produced a couple of fuses from the depths of his greatcoat. Ozzie dug out the holdall he was going to carry the dynamite in. Terry nodded his approval and Ozzie went to the fridge. A couple of minutes later, Ozzie had his greatcoat on too, and Terry was telling Gwyneth and Rose to wait at the flat for Red Mike and the others and they'd see them in the Glendower, the freaks' pub at the bottom of Bute Street, in an hour or so, as soon as they'd done their little bit of business.

It was only a ten-minute walk up to Tudor Road across the bridge and over to the station, but it felt a lot longer to Ozzie carrying a bag full of dynamite. Still, nothing untoward happened and soon the two hippies were walking along platform seven past the buffet and toilets and the signs telling travellers to go no further. At the end of the platform they jumped down next to the track and kept on walking for another thirty yards or so till they were on top of the railway bridge. It was a routine they'd done several times before. It was amazing how few people there were on the station on a Saturday lunchtime. On the wall next to the tracks you could see the signs of their previous visits, big white slogans – THE FIRE NEXT TIME, KICK OUT THE JAMS, FREE THE ANGRY BRIGADE. Terry had been planning on using the prime southern wall of the bridge for today's graffito but was annoyed to see he'd been beaten to it.

'Fuckin' IMG,' he said, surveying the words CHILE – VENCEREMOS. Then he walked a couple of yards further along, took out his aerosol can and began work on today's message – the one that would make the headlines. He began with a big R.

Meanwhile Ozzie walked up to the little coalhole-type structure they'd noticed on a previous spray-painting expedition, pulled open the wooden cover and found nothing there apart from a couple of dirty mags. Probably some railwayman's stash, thought Ozzie, as he deposited the dynamite on top of them. He waited for a moment till Terry finished his slogan, and the two of them walked back on to the platform just as one of the little valley's trains started to nose out of the station. No one appeared to have noticed a thing.

They were on to their second pint in the Glendower before the others turned up. Everyone in the pub was talking about the funeral. You'd think the Hammer had been some kind of spiritual leader to the assembled longhairs, not just that old blind black geezer used to play in the pubs and nobody paid him much notice.

'You hear it's going to be a New Orleans job?' someone asked Ozzie.

Ozzie nodded.

'Yeah. it's a local tradition,' said the guy, who had glasses and a hefty moustache and worked for some community film project, Ozzie thought, a suspicion confirmed a minute or two later when the guy said he had to shoot off and join his crew.

'Looks like there's going to be a film,' Ozzie said to Terry, striving to keep his voice neutral.

The others arrived in a cluster. Ozzie was pleased to see that Gwyneth had enough self-respect to keep her distance from Red Mike in public. Maybe it was just a one-nighter, he speculated, before catching himself in this train of excessively bourgeois sexual-jealousy bullshit.

Half an hour later – you didn't get Dafydd and Ken out of a pub in under half an hour – they were walking down Bute Street heading for the Casablanca. They had made it as far as the shops near Loudoun Square when Terry turned to Gwyneth and said, 'Where's the banner?'

Gwyneth looked quickly at Rose, then looked at Terry. 'Well, me and Rose were talking, we thought this isn't a march, right? It's supposed to be a funeral and maybe people wouldn't be too pleased seeing us with a banner. I mean, it's not a demo, is it?'

Terry looked mountainously pissed off for a moment but then he shrugged and said, 'No, you're right, wouldn't want to antagonise the community.'

It was half past two before they made it to the Casablanca, an old church turned reggae dancehall right down in the docks, but they were evidently in little danger of being late. There were a couple of big old hearses parked outside the club and a crowd of people milling about. Inside the Casablanca, the sound of a big jazz band tuning up could be heard. Ozzie

wandered in to have a look. In the centre of the room were a
bunch of white guys he recognised as the trad jazzers who
played at the Inn on the River, Sunday lunchtimes. Their
leader, a fat, white, bearded trombonist, was counting in the
inevitable 'When the Saints Go Marching In', focusing his
attention on a group of schoolkids carrying a motley assort-
ment of recorders, triangles, a violin and a couple of guitars.

'Just try and keep the beat. Don't worry too much about
the tune,' he was exhorting desperately. Ozzie stuck around
for a couple more run-throughs, and the sound was becoming
marginally less painful when the warm-up was interrupted by
a thunderous noise. In through the open door of the Casablanca came four black men dressed in African robes, their hair
in dreadlocks, carrying big African drums and beating them
with sticks.

The lead drummer came over to the trombonist.

'All right, Bev?' he said in a startlingly incongruous Cardiff
accent.

'Aye,' said the trombonist. 'All right, Barry, but what's with
the Zulu war drums?'

'Come to join the band, haven't we, Bev. Don't worry,
bra, you just keep with the jazz shit and we'll fit in.'

Bev shuddered but was just about to start things off one more
time when another party of new arrivals came in through the
door – evidently a local church choir. Bev looked about ready to
have a nervous breakdown. Ozzie slipped outside where he
found Terry in conversation with the film bloke and a local so-
called community leader, name of Big George.

'I thought these funerals were a local tradition,' said Ozzie,
'but it doesn't look like they've got a clue what's going on in
there.'

'Local tradition, man!' hooted Big George. 'Nah, man, some of the boys were in the Pilot the other night and they were talking about that James Bond thing, you know *Live and Let Die*. Wicked funeral at the beginning, seen. Thought the Hammer would have liked one of them.'

Ozzie could see the film guy backing off from the line of conversation, tuning it out. Local tradition was what he wanted, so a local tradition this funeral was going to be.

It was nearly four when the parade, now a couple of hundred strong, finally started moving. The drummers took the lead and, as the cortège wound through Mount Stuart Square, that was all you could hear, a huge growling beat. Then, as they came into James Street, the brass joined in, still playing 'When the Saints' but mutating it now to fit in with the drums. Bev had clearly reasoned that, with the drums, the rest of the band had to adapt or die. By the time they hit the long straight line of Bute Street, heading north towards the city centre, the schoolkids and the choir were in too and, while it was a bit of a racket, it was undeniably a mighty racket.

The procession was loosely split into mostly black locals at the front, and mostly white hippies and music lovers at the back. The South Wales Jazz Preservation Society was out in force, passing flagons of Brains Dark amongst themselves. The White Panthers were in the middle of things, forming a kind of flying wedge around the substantial figures of Dafydd and Ken, two blokes who, if you didn't know them to be a couple of harmless pissheads, looked like a pair of very mean bikers indeed. Ozzie was on the left of the wedge next to the diminutive blonde figure of Terry's old lady, Angie. Terry himself had already gone ahead on his mission.

Around halfway down the road, Ozzie began to get nervous. The band was playing a cacophonous but exhilarating version of 'The Rivers of Babylon', joints were being freely passed around from the front of the parade and bottles of beer from the back. The whole thing was starting to resemble a crazed seaside outing, but Ozzie couldn't keep his mind on it.

He and Terry had gone out to the Brecon Beacons a couple of weeks before and tried out setting off one stick of dynamite, using a fuse, and that had worked fine. Thirty seconds, just as it said in the *Cookbook*, plenty of time to get out of the way of the blast. But then the original plan had been to blow up the bridge in the middle of the night when no one was around, so a few seconds here or there wouldn't make much difference.

Now, however, Terry was going to try to time it so the bridge blew up in full view of the film camera. The risks suddenly looked huge. The bridge might come down on the marchers – almost impossible to justify, even with the most advanced revolutionary rhetoric – or it might take out an incoming train – which was also a little further than Ozzie was prepared to go.

Soon the bridge drew into sight, but the size of the procession – it had now swelled to nearly a thousand people – meant that it was just inching along the road. Ozzie could hardly bear it. At one point Gwyneth came over and asked if he was all right. 'Fine,' he said, 'fine, maybe a little too much reefer and booze in the sun.' She nodded and went back to Red Mike, who looked like he really was suffering from the sun and the booze, his face looking redder than his hair.

Fifty yards from the bridge, and Ozzie's nerves were at

screaming point. 'Do it now, you daft bastard,' he was inwardly shouting. 'How close do you want us to be?'

Twenty yards away from the bridge, and he was wondering whether he should run to the front of the parade and tell everyone to stop. As if they'd take any notice.

And then the front of the parade was under the bridge. Ozzie and the Panthers were still a further fifty yards behind, but Ozzie was starting to shake uncontrollably just waiting for the explosion. The question running through his mind was: 'Should I tell Gwyneth? Should I tell Gwyneth?'

He was just about to do so, he'd tapped her on the shoulder and was about to say something, when he realised it was already too late. They were under the bridge now.

Still, Gwyneth turned to him. 'What?'

'Oh,' he said, 'I was wondering if you'd seen Terry.'

'No,' she said, looking puzzled, 'I thought you knew where he was.'

'Yeah, well,' said Ozzie, weakly, 'I thought he'd be back by now.'

And that was it, they were through the bridge. Ozzie held his breath for a moment or two longer, waiting for the blast of rubble to hit them from behind as they carried on towards the town centre, but nothing happened. A train rumbled over the bridge and still nothing happened, and then Ozzie started to worry in earnest about Terry's whereabouts. Maybe he'd been nicked sneaking on to the bridge. Or maybe he'd just bottled the whole thing and headed for the pub.

And then Ozzie's attention was firmly dragged away from this line of thinking. Standing ahead of the funeral procession, a hundred yards or so beyond the bridge, near the beginning of the city's shopping centre, stood a line of police.

As the drummers approached the police Ozzie could see one of the policemen walk forward with his hand raised in the air, and start to talk.

Ozzie pushed forward so he could hear what was being said. The policeman was saying something about how there was no way an unlicensed demonstration could come into the city centre.

The lead drummer, the one named Barry, said, 'This ain't no demonstration. Supposed to be a funeral, man.'

The policeman just shook his head and said something Ozzie couldn't hear.

Barry turned around to the rest of the procession, which had grown ominously quiet since the band had stopped playing and the hearses hushed their motors.

Soon there was an angry muttering amongst the crowd that quietened only when the priest, a big red-faced rugby-playing type, walked forward to talk to the police. He spoke for a moment or two, started waving his arms around and then came back looking gloomy. He was about to say something when the first stone whistled past him and struck a copper right on the head.

Chaos broke out immediately. The police started forward, pulling out their truncheons. More stones were thrown, women clustered around the hearse started shrieking, and the scene looked set to get very ugly indeed, when there was a huge bang.

Everyone paused and looked back towards the noise. The sight that greeted their eyes was the Bute Street bridge slowly collapsing to the ground and, as the smoke and rubble cleared, there, on the far wall, now the only remaining part of the bridge, was the slogan 'Remember 1919'.

'Fookin' hell,' said the unmistakable voice of Red Mike in Ozzie's ear, 'nice one,' and suddenly they were running back towards the bombsite, ignoring the shouts of the police for everyone to remain calm and stay where they were. And it wasn't only Ozzie and the White Panthers who were running. Most of the Butetown youth were coming too, racing towards the rubble, clambering through it and over it, and into what suddenly seemed like the sanctuary of Butetown itself.

That evening the White Panthers got together at Gwyneth's house to watch it on the telly. There was no local news programme, this being a Saturday, but there it was, third story on the national news. First some shots of the aftermath and an interview with a couple of policemen condemning this reckless act of terrorism. Trains were indefinitely cancelled from Cardiff, passengers would have to use alternative bus services.

'Any idea who might be responsible?' the presenter asked. The camera focused in on the slogan 'Remember 1919'. No one seemed to have a clue what it meant. Somebody speculated that it indicated some kind of Welsh Nat solidarity with the Irish, and they'd got the date of the Easter Rising wrong. Terry swore and said they'd better get a communiqué out quickly.

'Any idea how the bomb was detonated?' the presenter asked. 'Yes,' said a policeman. 'A crude device, left somewhere on the bridge. The perpetrator or perpetrators would appear to have escaped by going further along the railway line and dropping down into some builders' yards via a rope.'

'Got that bit right at least,' grunted Terry.

The Glastonbury Arms

They got the communiqué out to the papers on Monday morning. None of the nationals seemed to take it seriously at first. But then a bloke named Randall on the *South Wales Echo* picked it up and made it a front-page splash, and by Tuesday lunchtime the Cardiff White Panthers were famous.

It was odd, really. Tuesday night, they all got together at what they called the Safe House, Ken's senile old uncle's place in Roath. They watched their news coverage and cheered, but they were basically terrified, sure the police would be through the door any second. Membership of the Panthers was meant to be kind of covert, but still it was hardly a secret amongst the people they knew. The next few days they stayed cooped up in the house, living on tins of tuna and driving each other mad.

Friday, Gwyneth had had enough and headed up to some cottage near Usk with one of the sisters. Saturday, Red Mike disappeared around six o'clock. Came back at two in the morning completely pissed. Said they'd been buying him drinks all night in the pub.

And by the next week they all gradually let their lives return to normal, as it became increasingly obvious that the Cardiff cops hadn't a clue how to go about catching a bunch of student revolutionaries.

Another month, and it was clear that they'd got away with it. Events in Ireland had long since blown the Panthers' exploit out of the news. The police had evidently given up and life returned imperceptibly to normal.

Some time in the summer they read a communiqué from Detroit: the American White Panthers had renounced violence. The group were horrified at first, but Ozzie was pretty sure he wasn't the only one who was secretly a little relieved that his career of terrorism looked to have come to a sudden end.

Still, they didn't give up activism, and, on a Friday night in late August, the six of them were out with spray cans on the Crwys Road bridge busily painting up the month's slogan – Carnival '76 Kick Out the Jams – when a single policeman, no more than nineteen years old, with an expression of utter terror on his face, walked up and told them they were breaking the law and he was putting them under arrest.

Red Mike laughed out loud, turned to the copper and said, 'Does your mother know you're out, son?' He was all set to deck the poor kid when Terry stepped in.

'No, Mike,' he said. 'Non-violence, remember.' Then he turned to the copper and said, 'OK, we're under arrest. Now, where d'you want to take us?'

'And that was the end of that,' said Ozzie.

Col laughed and shook his head and later on they walked outside and sat in the moonlight in the WNO car-park looking back at the bridge, sharing a smoke. After a while Ozzie laughed and Col looked round at him.

'Different times, man,' said Ozzie. 'Different times.'

The Casablanca

Tony Pinto came out of prison on a fine spring morning, wearing the same blue go-to-court suit he'd had on the day they convicted him. He came out the front door, turned right and crossed over the road to the lawyers' pub, Rumpoles. He knew Danny Jenkins, his so-called brief, would be in there. And so he was.

Tony went straight up to him, picked up a pint of lager from the table and tipped it over Danny's head. 'Start watching your back, Danny,' he said and walked out. No one said a thing.

Tony kept on going, into town, pleased that he could at least tick off item one from the checklist of things to do he'd built up over a year inside. And putting the fear of God into Danny Jenkins had had to be near the top. It was the principle of the thing. It wasn't that he'd expected Danny to get him off. God knows, he'd been caught bang to rights. But he'd thought a suspended wasn't out of the question, and if Danny had done the bare minimum – like showing up in court on time – then he might just have got that. Instead he ended up drawing two years, serving one.

A year, it was a weird length, just long enough for everything to change but not long enough for anything to look different. Walking into town now, it was like he'd never been away, and yet he knew nothing would be the same. He walked into a club, it wouldn't be the right club. He went to buy some new trainers, he wouldn't be sure which were the right ones. He went back to see his woman, he didn't know if she'd have him.

Tyra hadn't come to see him once while he'd been inside. She'd let his auntie come with the kids, she wasn't that heartless. But she had not been to see him once. It was his fault, of course; he'd broken something in her – in them – when he did the last stupid thing. After all the never evers he'd given her, all the times he'd promised no more bad-man business. And still he'd gone into the bookie's with his cousin. Billy waving a replica around like they were the sodding James Gang.

In no time he was at the corner of Bute Street. Question of whether to head on under the bridge, or into town. There was no reason to be in town, just the chance to be in a place full of people walking where they wanted, buying what they wanted, a place full of stuff. Not prison.

He decided it would probably just depress him, to be surrounded by citizens, so he took a deep breath and headed south under the bridge, to Butetown.

He was just passing the Custom House when out came a bloke, a hard, young bloke, and nearly bumped into him. Tony was ready in an instant. Bumping into people in prison was something you didn't do lightly. Then the guy spun and was halfway through saying sorry, boss, when they recognised each other. It was Mark, another of Tony's endless supply of cousins.

' 'Kin' 'ell, blood, you're out,' he said, clasping Tony's hand. 'You told Auntie Pearl?'

'No,' said Tony, 'thought I'd surprise her, like. Otherwise she'd have been down the prison waiting for me.'

Mark shook his head. 'Yeah, well.' Then he nodded towards the open door of the Custom House. 'Buy you a drink, bra?'

Tony shrugged. Why not, it had been a year since his last one. It wasn't that you couldn't get a drink inside, but he'd gone on a health kick the minute they banged him up. Just made it worse getting pissed inside.

They stood at the bar drinking bottles of Pils. There were just a handful of girls sitting inside, mostly the ones who were too old to make much of a go on the street, in the broad daylight anyway, just hung about in the Custom House for the company. Bobby was on the pool table as per. Some places, time really did seem to stand still.

'Like the new image,' said Mark.

Tony looked at himself in the mirror behind the bar. He'd lost a bit of excess weight while he'd been inside, his five-foot-ten frame looked lean and hard. He'd cropped his hair back to the bone and grown a little goatee, part of the Muslim kick. He hadn't gone for it all the way, but it was another thing to keep you sane inside. Still, seeing his reflection staring back at him, he was surprised to realise what a serious bastard he looked, 'specially wearing his suit, just needed a pair of little round glasses to complete the picture.

'So,' said Tony, after a little while, 'you seen Tyra?' He did his best to make it sound casual, but it obviously wasn't and Mark took a second before replying.

'Yeah, I seen her around. Picking up the kids from school, down the shop, them kind of places. She don't want much to do with me, though.'

Tony nodded; that figured.

'She's not been out clubbing or anything,' Mark went on. 'She's straight, your missis.'

Tony nodded again. That's why he didn't believe what he'd heard inside. He knew it was none of his business what she did anyway, way he'd let her down. But still he knew Tyra and he reckoned she'd wait till he was out before she started seeing anyone else. She liked things to be in the open. That was why he didn't believe what he'd heard about her and Mikey having a little scene. Fucking Mikey, he wouldn't put it past him to come sniffing round her yard, that's the way he was. Mate or not didn't mean nothing to Mikey, he thought he might get in there. But he couldn't see Tyra going for the little bastard.

'Least she's not been in here,' said Mark, and Tony wished he'd leave it alone. Of course Tyra wouldn't have been in the Custom House, she wasn't a hustler. It was time to move on, see what kind of a life he had left. He clashed fists with Mark and headed back out into the thin lunchtime sun.

Time to get it over with, go see Auntie Pearl. Auntie Pearl was his dad's sister and he'd lived with her after his mum had pissed off, back when he was ten. Twenty-three years ago now. They'd moved her into one of the new houses, right down in the docks past Techniquest, a good couple of years before he went inside, but it still felt odd to him, seeing her there.

She was thrilled to see him, of course, and he settled in and spent the afternoon, let her cook for him, put up with the stream of neighbours popping by to welcome him home. Relished them, really, because it meant that it was nearly six before there was a temporary lull and they were alone together, so Pearl could give him the third degree.

'I don't know,' he kept saying as Pearl asked him what he was going to do about Tyra. 'You don't know what she's like.'

Pearl was old-school stand by your man. Your man went to prison, you shrugged and cursed and got on with it and praised the lord when he came back out. You didn't bar the door to him. 'Go on,' she said, 'just go round there and ring on the door. The kids see you, she'll never throw you out.'

Christ, but old people were ruthless. 'No,' he said, 'I can't do that to her. She wants me back, I'll be back, I'm not going to force her. I'll see her tomorrow, when the kids are in school.'

'You stay here tonight?'

'Yes, Pearl,' he said, 'thanks,' and he got up, went over and hugged the old lady. It was a shock to realise it, but Pearl really was getting old now. 'I'll take a walk out now. Go see a few of the boys.'

'Oh,' she said, just as he was leaving, 'your cousin Billy called this afternoon. Wants you to call him back.' She paused a moment. 'You going to call him?'

Tony shook his head. 'Got nothing to say to him, Pearl.'

Pearl nodded and smiled, pleased.

Tony headed back up to James Street, thinking he might call in on Col, see what was happening. He cut up West Bute Street and then came to a stop outside Black Caesar's. He was meaning to have a look in the window of Kenny's clothes shop, and was staggered to see it had turned into a Nation of Islam mosque.

There'd been a lot of it about inside, a lot of the London brothers in particular, guys he'd hung around with when they'd had him down in Dartmoor for a while, they were well into it. But Kenny starting up a mosque, that was a career move and a half. Assuming this was Kenny's place, of course. The shop part at the front was closed but there was a light on out back so Tony leant on the bell for a little while. A minute later, there was Kenny himself, bigger than life as ever. Thing was, the moment Kenny caught sight of him, Tony could see his face tighten for a second. But then he opened the door and it was all how's it going, bra, when d'you get out?

After a moment Kenny stood back and looked at Tony. 'So, you checking the Nation of Islam?'

Tony gave a half-assenting shrug, and Kenny ushered him into the building. Showed him round the mosque which, to be honest, looked about three-quarters finished. Then they headed upstairs to the club, Kenny flicked a couple of lights on, brought a couple of beers from behind the bar and started boxing up a spliff.

'So, Ken, you got a lot of the boys coming down your mosque?'

Kenny shook his head. 'Long story, bra, long story. Thing is, I've got the mosque but we need a preacher.' The big man spluttered with laughter. 'You won't believe who we had try out preaching.'

Tony waited for the punchline.

'Mikey,' said Kenny, 'fucking Mikey Thompson. And, fair play to him, he gave it his best shot.' Then Kenny's mood seemed to darken. 'You seen your cousin?' he asked Tony.

'Which one?'

'Billy.'

Tony shook his head but Kenny carried on. 'I don't know what you've heard, but Billy's been a long way out of order.'

Tony raised his hands. 'Kenny, leave it. I don't want to know. I don't want to know anything about Billy. Last time I saw the cunt, I ended up in prison.' The irony of the thing was that, though the whole stupid business had been Billy's idea from start to finish, and though it had been Billy waving the damn replica around, it was Tony had ended up doing the time. Billy had walked 'cause some stupid fucking copper had compromised the identification. His witness, on the stand no less, had mentioned she'd had no trouble picking out Billy after the nice copper showed her his photo beforehand, 'just to jog my memory'. Far as Tony was concerned, though, Kenny could do what he liked with Billy.

Kenny leant forward, handed Tony the spliff.

'Safe,' said Tony, and the two of them sat there for another hour or so, talking about when they were kids. They were the same age, Kenny and Tony, and they'd played rugby together on the school team for a while – Kenny at centre, Tony at fly half – before Kenny got too good and went to play for Cardiff boys, and Tony got keener on chasing girls than standing round in the middle of a freezing bloody park, waiting to be clattered by some valleys retard as wide as he was high. Christ, it all seemed a long time ago now. And by the time they were eighteen, they'd both fucked up big time: Kenny had already been inside, and Tony had three kids by two different girls and was well into the hustling life.

Funny how they'd gone along in parallel, though: back then they'd both had dreadlocks, and now they were both wandering around looking like Malcolm X.

'Michael X,' said Tony, out of nowhere.

'Malcolm, you tosser,' said Kenny.

'No, no, there was a guy called Michael as well,' said

Tony. 'Trinidad fella, he was, like, the first British black Muslim.'

'Yeah?'

'Yeah, my dad knew him. He was on the boats, used to stay here sometimes.'

'Fuck,' said Kenny, and was quiet for a moment. 'What d'you reckon, I call it the Michael X Mosque?'

'Nice,' said Tony. 'Nice.'

Just then there was another blast on the bell and Kenny walked off to return a minute later with a middle-aged white guy.

'Tony,' he said, 'this is Bernie Walters.'

The guy stuck his hand out and Tony stood up to shake. He was one of those well-preserved specimens, looked fifty but was probably a good sixty, with a perma tan and a lot of gold, round his neck, on his fingers, though the sharp blue suit was classier than the rest of him.

Thing was, though, you looked hard at Bernie Walters and the word 'bent' came fast back at you. Tony decided to leave them to it. 'Ta for the drink, Ken,' he said, and Kenny just waved, already busy talking to Walters. Something to do with hiring exotic dancers for the lunchtime trade. Tony wasn't sure what Walters's involvement was; the last words he heard him say were, 'Not like the old days, Ken, remember the girl with the snake?'

Tony walked out, holding a laugh back. The girl with the snake had to be his Auntie Deandra. She'd been something else when he was a kid. Been an extra in Tiger Bay when she was just a kid herself and showbiz had certainly got in the blood. Times he remembered seeing her, she was always wearing a fur coat, and he had thought she was a film star. But there was shame and scandal in the family, he remembered that. Long time till he found out why. The original exotic dancer – Deandra and the snake. Christ.

Out on the street, he realised he'd been longer than he thought in Black Caesar's, it was getting on for nine now. He hurried round to Col's place but there was no one in. He carried on to the Paddle and it was deader than ever, just a handful of old-timers watching TV; he ducked out again before any of them could collar him, and wondered where to go next. He was just heading down Angelina Street, thinking to give Mikey a call, when he realised he was passing Mandy's place.

On the spur of the moment, he rang on the bell and seconds later there she was, her dark-blonde hair dragged back from her forehead and held in a ponytail, looking trim as ever, never an extra pound on her. He remembered when she was a kid she was always winning the long-distance running prizes.

'Christ,' she said, 'look what the cat dragged in.' Then she got up on tiptoe and threw her arms round him.

'You seen Pearl yet?' she said after a moment.

Why did everyone keep asking him that? 'Yeah,' he said, 'I just escaped now.'

They laughed together. That was their bond. Pearl had taken them both in as kids, Tony as a ten-year-old after his mum left and his dad couldn't cope with him on his own. Then Mandy a couple of years later, after her dad fucked off wherever it was he fucked off to and her mum went to pieces. So she'd been like a kid sister to him for a time.

Sitting down in the front room, he played with the two little girls, Emma and Brittany, for a while before Mandy packed them off to bed.

Mandy boxed a draw then and Tony lay back on the sofa, his eyes idly resting on *Friends* on the TV, savouring the sensation of not being in prison.

'How's your love life then, Mand?' he asked eventually.

Mandy made a face. 'Don't ask,' she said, and then, before Tony had more than an instant in which not to ask, she told him anyway. 'You won't believe who I had a scene with, Tone.'

Tony raised his eyebrows obligingly.

'Only Jim Fairfax, you remember Jimmy?'

'You talking about the Jimmy Fairfax that's in the police?'

Mandy nodded.

'Fuckin' hell, Neville must have been pleased.'

'That's what I thought, Tone. I was busy running round trying to hide it – turns out Neville and Jimmy are best fucking mates, you know what I mean. Doing a little bit of business.'

Tony whistled, shook his head.

'I'm sick of it, Tone. You know what I'd like, one time in my life, see some bloke you don't spend your whole time wondering when the police are going to come round middle of the night, kick your door in.'

She broke off. Tony had put his hands in the air. 'Ah, sorry, Tone,' she said. 'How'd it go this time, anyway?'

'No,' he said, 'you're right, I've had enough of it and all.'

'Yeah, well,' said Mandy, and fetched a couple of cans of Coke from the fridge. They sat for a while in amiable silence watching one of those American sitcoms where some glamorous blonde runs around pretending her life's in a mess when it obviously isn't.

Next thing Tony knew, it must have been about midnight.

He woke up from a vivid dream about being back in prison and felt a sense of exquisite joy to find himself lying on Mandy's sofa with a blanket over him. The TV was still on but Mandy didn't seem to be watching it. She had her nose in a library book, one of those old-time tales of plucky mill girls and orphan boys.

He watched her for a moment, his eyes just barely open, then stretched and sat up and said, 'Mand, did Pearl ever tell you where my mum went?'

'No,' said Mandy, 'don't think I ever heard her say anything 'bout your mum, except to curse her now and again. Didn't she run away to be a big star?'

Tony reached over for his can of Coke, swirled it around a bit before taking a sip, and then said, 'Yeah, something like that.'

'What was her name?'

'Fatima.'

'No, her singing name.'

'April,' said Tony after a while, 'April Angel. Stupid, yeah?'

'No,' said Mandy, 'I think it sounds good.' Then she went quiet a moment before saying, 'Tell you what, Tone, I've an idea who might know something.'

'Who?'

'This bloke runs clubs, he's been running clubs for ever. He's going partners with Kenny Ibadulla, doing up the Casablanca.'

'Oh yeah, what's his name?'

'Bernie. Bernie Walters.'

'Shit, I seen him today.'

'How come?'

'I was round Caesar's with Kenny. Bloke with a lot of rope,

looks like he lives under a sunbed, comes in. That's the guy, yeah?'

Mandy nodded.

'So what's he want with the Casa?'

'Want to open it up again, put bands on and stuff, get the students down.'

'So what's he want with Kenny?'

'Well, Kenny's the man, case you hadn't noticed. He does all right with Caesar's, and I suppose Bernie needs him for security and that, saves paying him to do it, anyway Kenny comes in as a partner.'

Tony nodded. That made sense. It had been one of Kenny's main rackets for years, charging anyone opened up down the docks for a bit of security. Security from Kenny mostly. Few of the boys didn't mind causing a little trouble, Kenny asked them to nicely, like. So, yeah, he could see it made sense, bring Kenny in the front door for a change, save him knocking your back door down with a baseball bat.

'And this Bernie, how d'you know him?'

'DJing. Been playing records one of his clubs in town, the Los Angeles. Been playing out there every Thursday. You should come down, like, few of the boys, show up most nights. But, Tone, what's this about your mum anyway?'

'Nah, nothing, Mand, just prison bollocks. Too much time staring at the wall.'

'What, you been thinking 'bout trying to contact her?'

'No,' said Tony. 'Leave it, Mand, really.'

'All right,' she said. 'Still, tell you what, tomorrow night there's going to be special benefit night down the Casa, they're opening up for one night only, some kind of charity thing before they open it up proper next month. I'll be playing there, and Delroy, and there's some guys meant to be coming down from London. And Bernie'll be there. Got to be there, Tony. Back on the scene.'

'Maybe I have, Mand, or maybe I don't.'

'What's that supposed to mean?'

'Wish I knew, Mand. Wish I knew.' And, with that, Tony, his mood suddenly plummeting, got up and headed back to Aunt Pearl's. He hesitated for a moment outside Caesar's, then thought sod it, he'd see everyone tomorrow.

Next morning was a blow-out. He'd been planning to go over to see Tyra while the kids were at school, but like a twat he'd forgotten it was a Saturday, so he belled her instead and it was like talking to an iceberg. I'm out, he'd said, like she might be pleased. I know, she'd said, and it had gone downhill from there. Eventually she said he could come round Monday morning, like it was some big favour.

He didn't even dare ask about the kids, and after he put the phone down he just sat there for a while in Auntie Pearl's front room, grateful that the old lady had gone off up town shopping, sat there doing his very best to think of nothing at all.

Then he shook himself out of it and picked up the phone again. Called Mikey at home and got Tina, who was in a decent mood for once, gave him a mobile number. Couple of tries and he got Mikey himself, sounding like he was talking from the middle of a building site. And he wasn't sure whether it was the line or not, but he could have sworn he heard a note of fear in Mikey's voice when he realised it was Tony. Anyway, Mikey said he'd see him down the Ship about one.

Tony was halfway through his first pint when Mikey showed up, which was par for the course.

'How's it going, bra?' said Mikey, sitting himself down, no sign of the nervousness Tony thought he'd detected over the phone. 'Christ, you turned into a Jehovah's Witness or what?'

Tony laughed: for some reason he'd put a suit on again today. He'd just stared at the pile of Nike stuff lying in his room round at Pearl's and it had suddenly struck him that all that wasn't him any more. Walking round advertising some Babylonian corporation. So he'd suited up.

'Yeah, well,' he said, 'I hear you've turned preacher and all, Mikey.'

'One time, bra, one time only, and only that time 'cause Kenny would have ripped my throat out I said no. Never felt such a twat in my whole life. You hear about what happened?'

Tony nodded.

Mikey laughed. 'You should have seen Kenny's face, man, he realised those Brummies had put that one over him. Thought he was going to explode.' Then Mikey's tone changed. 'You've heard about your cousin?'

Tony shook his head.

'Your cousin Billy, he's heading for a war with Kenny, and Kenny's been so pissed off since then, he's most likely going to give him one.'

'What?'

'Yeah. Billy's started thinking he's Mister Untouchable ever since he got off that bookie's thing with you – reckons he can get away with anything if he can get away with waving a shooter in a bookie's.'

'Fake shooter,' said Tony.

'Yeah, well, ever since then he reckons he's the ranking don in person. You hear about him waving a shooter around in the street some other Birmingham crew came down?'

'I haven't heard nothing, Mikey. I've been inside, you hadn't noticed.'

'Yeah, well, being inside doesn't mean you don't hear things.'

There was a sudden silence, as Tony recalled what he had heard inside. Tyra and Mikey. He still didn't believe it, but the little man was looking mighty shifty again.

'So where've you been this morning?' asked Tony, by way of changing the subject.

'Nowhere much, just a little bit of work for Kenny getting the Casa ready for tonight. You hear about tonight?'

'Yeah.'

'Coming down?'

'Yeah.'

'Cool, bra,' said Mikey, standing up, 'I'll check you later then.' Then, as he was leaving, he turned and added, 'You know Billy's put the word out. Wants you to get in touch. Urgent, like.'

'Yeah, yeah,' said Tony.

Tony sat there for a while longer. Momentarily he felt at a complete and utter loss. The world had been spinning for a full year while he had been staring at the walls and doing push-ups on the floor, and now the speed of the spin was too much. He'd been here before, of course. This had been the fourth time he'd been inside. Fucking good thing he wasn't in California or they'd have thrown away the key. 'Course, they'd been in California, cousin Billy would have been waving a real shooter and . . .

And it didn't bear thinking about. But he had to think about Billy. Had to find out what kind of war Billy was planning with Kenny before he got caught in the middle of it.

And it might as well be now, he thought, fuck all else to do Saturday afternoon, every other bastard out shopping with the missis. Good a time as any for a trip out to Ely. Billy would be in, he was sure; Billy wasn't the shopping type. Leastways, not unless he was carrying a sawed-off.

Out of the pub, Tony decided to walk to the bus station. Passed Kenny's mosque on the way. The shop was open this time and a fit-looking sister inside reading something called *Men Are From Mars*. She looked up and waved when she saw Tony, and Tony waved back but didn't go in, seemed like his motor wasn't running yet. Instead he studied a notice pinned to the window, promising a meeting two p.m. tomorrow, Sunday, with Cyrus talking about Black Men and Nature: the Hidden Truth.

It started to rain, a sudden quick shower, as he walked down Bute Street. Suited Tony fine, meant every old biddy with nothing better to do didn't stop and talk to him and make him promise to never do anything bad again 'less he wanted to see Auntie Pearl in her grave. That, and it was just a pleasure to be out in the weather, feel the rain on your face.

Bus station, he picked up a *Mirror* and sat on the bus reading the football pages while he waited for it to get moving. Twenty minutes later, the bus dumped him on Cowbridge Road, just opposite the big snooker club, and he walked up on to Grand Avenue. Christ, there was something so fucking depressing about Ely. The houses were all grey pebbledash, and way it was stuck up on the hillside made the wind whip though it like a buzzsaw. About two shops in the whole place, shopkeepers behind full-length security grilles, and everywhere you looked bored youth just checking for something or someone to do. He was just coming up to Billy's place, right on Grand Avenue, and a couple of kids, couldn't have been more than eighteen, stared at him.

'Oi, cunt,' the fat one said. And was about to follow up when Tony turned into Billy's yard.

'Oh sorry, mate,' the porker said then. 'Didn't know you were –'

'Were what?'

'Friend of Billy's.'

Tony didn't say anything, just gave them the old prison stare. Christ, it was worrying, though, little twats like that didn't give you any respect. Then he looked down at himself, kept forgetting he was wearing a suit.

Tony knocked on the door and Billy's woman, Stacey, opened up. She was a washed-out-looking blonde; Tony knew for a fact she couldn't be more than twenty-five, but she'd have passed for forty any day. What living with Billy Pinto did for you.

Billy was in the front room watching Sky Sports with the curtains drawn, Simply Red playing on the sound system.

He half turned at the sound of a newcomer, then leapt up when he saw who it was.

Billy gave the situation all the necessary. How sorry he was it had all screwed up, how it should have been Tony got off and not him, blah, blah, blah. Tony felt like he'd floated out of his body and was just up there on the ceiling, watching this go on.

'Want one of these?' said Billy after a bit, pointing at a pile of boxed PlayStations in the corner of the room. 'Go on, bra, take one.'

Tony shook his head. Billy looked at him bemused, suddenly registering Tony's suit.

'Whassup, Tone, you gone Muslim? Allah told you fucking computer games are no good for the soul?'

'Billy,' said Tony, suddenly tired, 'what's happening with you and Kenny?'

Billy stepped back, all trace of the geniality gone now. Actually, Tony preferred him that way. He'd known his cousin was a psycho since they were kids, and he'd always hated dealing with nice-guy Billy 'cause you spent the whole time waiting for bad-boy Billy to come out. Least once he was like that you knew where you were.

'Who you been talking to, Tone?' he asked now.

'Kenny.'

'Fuck you talking to Kenny for?'

'He's my mate, butt, been my mate since we were kids. Been your mate too. Last thing I knew, before I went down the bookie's for a year, you were still mates. I comes out. I walks past his mosque, which is another thing I'm not expecting, and I sees Kenny, and he calls me in, boxes a draw and we talk about this and that. He says you're going to war with him. And now I comes here to find out what's going on before you dump me in it again.'

Billy stared at Tony. 'Money, Tone, money. What d'you think it's about? Kenny's had it all his own way too long. Just 'cause he's big he thinks he's bad, and all the other clowns follow along behind him. Kenny tells them to walk like an Egyptian, they'll all be wearing fezzes, you know what I mean. And it's like there's a ton of gear coming through Cardiff at the moment; the boat comes in from Trinidad, there's more fucking Charlie than bananas on it, like.

'And it's time someone else got a piece of the action. Load of the stuff goes straight up to London. Some firm comes down, sorts it out, it's all locked down tight. But there's enough other shit around, and I'm sick of buying it all off Kenny. I've got the business round here,' he waved out the window, 'Kenny knows that, but long as I'm buying off him he's laughing anyway. Time Kenny moved over, let someone else have a share.'

'And how are you going to do that? Kenny got a lot of boys he can call on. Who you got?'

'Got a few boys up here, don't mind getting stuck in. Got some friends up Birmingham interested in making a deal, guys don't like Kenny one little bit. There's a boat coming in next week. Wednesday night. That's when it's going to happen, Tone. That's when I'm going to let Kenny know the rules have changed. And now I've got my cousin Tony, back out of prison. Only brer I ever seen Kenny back off a fight with.'

'That's 'cause I had a knife and he didn't.'

'Wouldn't stop Kenny most times, most people don't know how to use a blade, Tone.'

'Yeah, well, that's not me any more.'

Tony turned away as Billy shot him a sour look. 'Oh sorry, Tone, forgot you'd turned into Louis fucking Farrakhan since you been inside.'

'Anyway, what I hear, Kenny's going legit. This club business and all. Taking over the Casa. You heard about this business guy he's going in with?'

'Who's that?'

'Bloke name Bernie Walters.'

'Bernie Walters,' said Billy slowly, his eyes narrowing. 'I heard that name.'

'Yeah, well, he's supposed to own some club up town.'

'No, that's not it. It was a long time ago. Bernie Walters. Something my mum told me. He's an old guy, yeah?'

'Yeah,' said Tony. 'Anyway, forget Bernie Walters, Billy, and forget hauling me into your thing with Kenny. You want to play ranking gangsters with big Ken, go on. Just leave me out.'

'Yeah.'

'Yeah,' said Tony, and got up to go.

As he was leaving, Billy shouted after him, 'I'll be seeing you, Tone. Ask your missis. Ask your missis what Kenny made her do. Then tell me you're staying out of it. Wednesday night, Tone. Wednesday night.'

Tony kept on walking, like he never heard a word.

Tony made it to the Casablanca around midnight. He'd come out of Billy's house with his head reeling, just thinking it was time to get out of Cardiff, to get out of his life. And then his mind started running round in circles. Sure he could get out of Cardiff, 'cept he'd have to leave his woman, leave the kids, leave Auntie Pearl. And of course he could go up to London and stay with some of the friends he'd made inside. Friends he'd made inside – he repeated that to himself, letting the implications sink in. Yeah, he could go up to London and find himself in the same gangster business he was running away from down here. Fucking Billy, fucking Kenny, why couldn't people just let you live your life? He was seriously thinking of going to work on the boats by the time he got back to Auntie Pearl's.

He'd gone out that evening in a filthy bloody mood, but the strange thing was he'd been having a really good time. Played some pool in the Avondale with a few of the boys. Little drink, little smoke, and Tony was feeling just nicely blocked up as he walked into the Casa.

The Casablanca was an old church down in Mount Stuart Square, right in the heart of the docks' business district. It had been a dancehall as long as Tony could remember, except for being closed the last five years or so.

Walking in the door, it was like a violent attack of déjà vu. Here was Mikey on the door, done up in his tux the way he always used to, looking like that little bloke from the Stylistics. Standing in the lobby talking to Mikey, who looked a lot more chipper than he had done at lunchtime, he could have sworn he heard some serious dub playing inside. Remembered different times, the late seventies, early eighties, him and Mikey and Kenny and Billy and all the rest, just kids all of them, trying to grow locks. Mikey had the best; later on he had them piled up high in a tam, made him look taller. Reckoned that was a lot of the charm of Rastafari for Mikey – big hair and a staff and all the draw you could take. Dancing with Tyra to lovers' tunes. 'Caught You In a Lie.'

Where did the time go? He shook his head. He knew it was all bullshit; there never were any good old days. Pushed open the door into the main hall and came sharply back into the present. Hardstep drum and bass all the way. Room full of kids like he used to be, youth trying to look tough, girls trying to look tough and sweet at the same time.

Trouble with this hardstep shit, Tony thought, was you couldn't dance to it. All you could do was pose to it. Sounded all right – in fact sounded great – in the car, driving round with the big bass speakers making the whole motor shake and old ladies cover their ears. But in a club on a Saturday night, you wanted something a little sweeter.

'All right, Tone,' said a voice at his ear. Mandy. 'Tyra not coming down with you?'

He bent down, shouted in her ear, 'No, haven't seen her yet.'

Mandy mimed disappointment, then pointed over at the decks. 'Time I did some work. Later on, Tony.'

He nodded, walked over to the bar, where the sound was a little less ear-splitting. Col was there, and he and Tony clashed fists and bullshitted around a little, talking about the Glastonbury Wars.

The Glastonbury Festival for years had been like Christmas to the Butetown boys. You could sell whatever you could get your hands on to the million students in the mud. By the end of the weekend you'd be selling aspirins, Beechams Powders, bags of toffees, anything you could lay your hands on looked remotely like a controlled substance. Or at least looked like one to someone who'd spent the last three days discovering whether scrumpy and acid really are the perfect match.

First few years it had been great, they'd had the place virtually to themselves. Lately it had got like strategic warfare. Crews from all over the country were trying to get in on the action, people turning up days beforehand staking out their territory, shooters everywhere. Free-market economics and no mistake.

After a while Col headed off into a corner to do a little bit of business and Tony drifted back into the main hall. The mood had got mellower since Mandy took over the decks, mixing in some deep house and garage with a little swing to keep the girls happy. She caught Tony's eye as he walked across the floor; he nodded back, noticing a little jolt of excitement that went through him at her smile. Just then he caught sight of Kenny heading towards the backstage area. Tony raised an arm and Kenny waved him over. Made a follow-me sign and headed backstage.

There was nothing much there, a shambolic space full of bits of old speakers and similar crap, a little bathroom cum dressing-room over in the corner and a table at the back. Sitting at the table were Bernie Walters and another white guy, a heavy-set thirtyish type in a suit, looked like he might be ex-army. Respectable-looking type, but respectable muscle is still muscle and that's what this guy was, you could see it a mile off. 'Come on, Tone,' said Kenny, 'say hello to the gents.'

'Bernie,' he said, 'this is Tony Pinto, feller I was telling you about, said hello to you in Caesar's yesterday.'

Tony nodded like an idiot, as if he was confirming his own existence. Christ, he was thinking, was that only yesterday?

'Good to meet you again, son,' said Bernie, standing up to shake Tony's hand. 'Been hearing good things about you from Ken here.'

Tony nodded again, his mind racing through a fog of drink and smoke, wondering what the hell this was all about.

'Tell you what,' said Bernie, seemingly impervious to Tony's silence, 'here's my card. How about you come and have lunch with me Monday? I've got a proposal you might be interested in. One o'clock OK?'

Tony stayed silent for a moment longer. This simply wasn't how things were done in his world. People didn't make lunch appointments with you. Still, God knows he had nothing to lose. 'All right,' he said.

'Good,' said Bernie, 'I'll see you then,' and then he turned and started talking to Kenny. After a moment Tony realised he'd been dismissed and headed back into the dancehall.

Delroy was at the controls now and Tony saw that the crowd had changed. There seemed to be fewer young people around and more of the old crew. Delroy was pumping out classic funk tunes. The big synth bass of 'Just Be Good to Me' boomed out and Mandy was there tapping him on the arm. 'Fancy a dance then?'

Suddenly it was three in the morning and Tony was walking out of the Casablanca, with Mandy, walking her home. But the weather had cleared and it was a glorious spring night, and instead they headed down to the waterfront, through the midst of the bay development. Stood together for a while by the Norwegian church talking about the way it had all been when they were kids. The places that weren't there any more and the things that had replaced them. The usual nostalgic shit. At one point they had their heads right together leaning over the sea wall and Tony felt the urge to kiss her but he pulled back. Like a sister to him, that kind of feeling. Thing people always said when they meant they didn't fancy someone, but this time it was true.

Tony slept right through to lunchtime. Woke up momentarily at half six, opened his eyes for long enough to register he wasn't in prison any more, and shut them again. Next thing he knew, it was half one and he could hear Auntie Pearl and a couple of the church ladies having lunch in the next room.

They were still there when he emerged half an hour later, wearing the grey suit he'd bought for Tyra's brother's wedding. Nice suit but he'd hardly worn it since. It was becoming a thing for him, though, he realised, not to get back into the sports. Wasn't the way he wanted to be any more. What was, though? That was the question.

The old ladies were thrilled, of course, started talking about the old days, you never saw a man except in a suit. He sat down with them for a while, ate some rice and peas, then, when he could stand it no longer, he remembered something. 'See you later, ladies,' he said, 'I've got a meeting to go to.'

There were half a dozen people inside the mosque when he got there, waiting for Cyrus's talk. A couple of old dreads, Clyde and Paulie, Twelve Tribes brethren. Tony wasn't sure whether they were checking out the competition or what. A couple of younger guys, maybe he'd seen them around, he wasn't sure; they both looked keen, one of them had brought his girlfriend, who looked anything but. And there in the corner, talking to Cyrus himself, was Col. Tony raised his fist in greeting but didn't go over. Cyrus was one of those people you didn't want to get stuck with. He was an older bloke; hard to say how old but he'd known Tony's dad and he'd been the first person Tony remembered seeing around with locks. Weird thing was he'd always tell you he wasn't a Rastafarian, some kind of mutant Christian instead. Anyway, he was always wandering round the pubs testifying about this and that and he was all right, but you had to be in the mood for him.

Still, he was taking the lecture seriously. Three o'clock precisely, he closed the door, moved to the front of the room, stepped up behind the lectern – Tony couldn't help laughing at the thought of Kenny shopping around for a lectern – and started talking. Black men and nature was his subject and it was one he rapidly warmed to.

Tony'd heard it all before, but he didn't mind; there was something relaxing about listening to the old dread explain that black men were essentially a higher, more physically evolved species than white men, a point illustrated by the potent comparison between the achievements of Butetown's own world-beating Colin Jackson and those of the entire Welsh rugby team. The scientific rationale for this revolved around an extra gland found in black men but not white men, Cyrus explained.

Tony couldn't help wondering what that meant for most of the people in Butetown who, like him, were mixed race. He didn't have to wait long for an answer, though; Cyrus had clearly been asked this enough times. 'The white gene is a recessive gene,' he boomed. 'If black and white mix, the black wins out. Nah true?'

All present were happy enough to say amen to that, and Cyrus moved on to the second part of his thesis, which was that black men were not just better fitted out by nature but also had a closer relationship to nature. Whole thing built up to the usual exhortation to return to Africa and farm the ancestral soil, and Tony smiled and nodded and drifted away under the influence of Col's wickedly strong homegrown. He was transported to his kitchen back when he was a kid, listening to his dad and his mates sit around with a few bottles of the Export Guinness, the Nigerian stuff, setting the world to rights.

Seemed like a different life, thinking about it now: that kid, a lanky ten-year-old who played rugby, for Christ's sake, a different kid. His mum – still there. His dad – still alive.

Wandering off after the meeting, he found himself thinking about his mum again. Trying to figure out what the hell happened. A woman walks out one day, never comes back. The weird thing, thinking about it now, was that he'd never asked where she went. No one talked about her at all. His dad and Auntie Pearl, they'd done it on purpose, he supposed; had the idea it was best not to talk about her.

Before long he found himself back at Mandy's place. She was there with a friend, girl named Gail, four kids running round the house causing mayhem. Mandy was pleased to see him, though, and they ended up taking the kids out for a little walk down the playground. It was the wrong thing to do, really. Seeing Mandy was good, but playing with other people's kids just brought it home how much he'd thrown away. And he didn't stay long, headed back to Auntie Pearl and an evening watching TV, little glass of rum before bedtime. Billy called a couple of times but Pearl told him Tony was out. Apparently he'd been calling all day.

Next morning he was round to Tyra's by ten. She opened the door, looked at him, her expression giving nothing away, and ushered him into her front room – *their* front room last time he'd been in it. He just stood there looking round, staring at the children's toys scattered around the place, and suddenly Tyra came to him, pulled him to her, threw her arms around his neck. And they stood there hugging for what seemed like minutes. Then she broke off and without a word headed for the bathroom. He waited five minutes – he was watching the clock this time – and she came out, and he sensed the difference immediately. Pure chill was radiating at him now. They sat down, him on the sofa, her on the chair.

'What are you going to do now, Tony?' she asked. 'Go see cousin Billy, see if he's got another little job for you?'

'No,' he said, 'I . . .'

'You what? You're going to stop messing about the gangster business, come back here, be a real dad to your kids? You going to get a job? You wouldn't know where to start. You know where the job centre is, Tony? You goes into town, it's on Charles Street, big fucking orange place. You goes in there, they gives you a job working in the petrol station, two fifty an hour. 'Cept they won't let you do it 'cause they'd think you'd rip off the fucking till. And they'd be right.'

Tony just sat there, his head bowed, taking it. He knew what other people would do, what they'd say. Tell him to give her a slap. Not just men, that's what women told you too. Don't take that shit, give her a smack. Got to make her respect you. What his dad believed, all right. Shit, something he didn't want to think about snagged on the corner of his mind and receded again. Whatever, it wasn't him; he couldn't lay a finger on Tyra. He didn't feel good about it, knew he'd hurt her already worse than any slap. So he just sat there taking it.

'Look at you,' she said. 'You comes in here wearing a suit. You know the last man came round here wearing a damn suit?'

Tony shook his head.

'A fucking bailiff, that's who it was. He was going to take the TV, the video right under the kids' faces.'

'What d'you do?' asked Tony.

'I called my man, didn't I? 'Cept he was in Dartmoor. What d'you think I did? Asked the man how much, then I called Kenny. Kenny comes round, gives the guy two hundred. And then I owed Kenny. Then I owed fucking Kenny.'

She lost it then, threw herself across the room at Tony, started hitting him, drumming her fists on his chest. Then, just as suddenly, she stopped, went to the bathroom again, this time for no more than a minute. She didn't sit down again when she came out.

'Just go now,' she said. And Tony, feeling numb, just stood up, straightened his jacket.

He looked straight at Tyra for a moment, thought about saying something like I'm sorry and rejected it, thinking it sounded pathetic. Instead he just headed for the door.

'Don't you want to see your kids, then?'

Tony turned and looked at her again. He still couldn't make any words come out. Finally he managed to make himself nod.

'All right,' she said, 'I'll bring 'em round your auntie's, tomorrow after school.'

Walking away, Tony felt a sudden wave of anger, an onrush of how-dare-the-bitch-talk-to-me-like-that fury. And, just as suddenly, that too receded, to be replaced by something too near to despair for Tony to want to look at it too closely. Instead he concentrated on putting one foot in front of the other, heading back to Auntie Pearl's until he remembered he had a lunch appointment.

Bernie Walters's office turned out to be right in the middle of town, the top end of St Mary Street, one of the big old Gothic buildings there. Downstairs was a coffee importer's. Bernie's office was on the first floor. Seemed like a pretty minimal operation to Tony: a secretary in the front office, a couple of accountant types in the middle office, then Bernie himself in a great big office looking out over the street. Bernie was putting his coat on as Tony entered.

'You're late, son.'

Tony shrugged, like he could care less, morning he'd had. Anyway, he'd seen the time in the secretary's office. Ten past. Guy should see late some time.

'You asks me to come here, I'm here. You wants me to go, I'll go.'

'No,' said Bernie, shaking his head. 'Sorry, son, just been one of those days so far. Let's go and eat.'

They walked together up to the top of St Mary Street and round the corner to the little strip where a bunch of restaurants had started putting tables outside on the pavement. Bernie bypassed the first couple of places, then turned into the next one, some kind of Italian joint. Tony followed him in, watched as Bernie went through a backslapping routine with the guy with the are-you-serious Italian accent by the bar, and then they headed to a booth right at the back.

Even then, they didn't get down to business. Instead Bernie started fussing about with the menu, talking to Tony as if he'd never eaten in a bloody restaurant before, ordering a bottle of wine then looking pissed off when Tony asked for a Coke.

'What's this all about?' Tony asked, once the waiter had finally disappeared and the drinks arrived.

'Look,' said Bernie, 'what I do is I run clubs. Been running clubs around town since the fifties when I was a kid myself.'

Tony nodded.

'Right then,' Bernie went on, 'then you've probably heard. I'm going into business with Kenny Ibadulla, get the Casablanca going again.'

Tony nodded once more and switched off while Bernie went into a spiel about what a great asset to the bloody community it would be having the Casa open again. For a moment Tony thought he was going to ask him to invest in the damn place. 'What's it to do with me?' he asked finally, as Bernie started to slow up.

'Well,' said Bernie, 'me and Kenny have been thinking.

We need someone to manage the club. Kenny's got Caesar's to look after and I'm all over the place, so we need someone on the spot. Someone knows how things work, and we can trust not to stick all the money in their own pocket.' Bernie paused and smiled a smile that didn't even think about reaching his eyes. 'And let's just say that you come highly recommended.'

Tony sat back for a moment, tried to get his head round this, then leaned forward again. 'Bullshit,' he said, 'I just got out of prison Friday, turning over a bookie's. Now you want me managing your club. Don't even nearly add up.'

Bernie leant back now but he was smooth, Tony couldn't read what was going on behind his eyes. 'Yes,' he said finally. 'I heard about that. Kenny told me you'd been in trouble. And I took the liberty of looking into it a bit. Line of work like mine, you make a few contacts in the police force, as you can imagine.' He paused for a moment for Tony to imagine the kind of police contacts Bernie was talking about. The kind of contacts showed up at your club in the afternoon asking for a bag of money to make sure the health and safety don't look too hard, or you don't get busted for under-age drinkers or drugs in the toilets. Contacts. Made the world go round.

'Anyway,' Bernie carried on, 'I made a couple of calls. And I found out something rather interesting. Let me ask you this, Tony. Did you ever wonder why you ended up doing time and not your cousin Billy who, after all, as I understand it, was the one with the gun?'

'Replica,' said Tony automatically.

'Replica, then. Didn't you ever wonder why he didn't get sent down?'

Tony looked at Bernie hard, seeing exactly what he was

suggesting. 'Police screwed up the case, didn't they? Their witness fucked them up on the stand. Otherwise he'd been doing five years at least.'

'Hmm,' said Bernie, 'convenient that, wasn't it, witness screwing up like that.'

'Look,' said Tony, 'stop pissing about. You telling me Billy grassed me up? Don't see it myself. They'd have had me anyway. Didn't need to give him anything.'

'Yeah, well, Tony, sorry to tell you this, but what my sources say is your cousin Billy talks to the trees on a regular basis, right old whispering grass.'

Tony sat back for a moment, trying to let this compute. Did he believe it? Maybe. Billy was a cunt any way you looked at him, and a lying cunt at that, always had been. Question was, though, who cared? 'So what?' he said to Bernie. 'What's any of this to do with you?'

'Well,' said Bernie, 'I don't think it'll be news to a bright boy like you if I tell you that your cousin Billy and my associate Mr Ibadulla are not on the best of terms. In fact I'm reliably informed that Billy is planning to attempt to move in on Kenny's, shall we say, private business. You follow me?'

Tony nodded. ' 'Course I follow you. Thing I don't see is what it's got to do with me. I got nothing to do with Billy.'

'Not exactly what I've heard, Tony.'

Tony stared at him.

'What I heard, Tony, you went to see cousin Billy on Saturday afternoon.'

Christ, thought Tony, how the hell could he have known that? And started to realise that whatever was going on was a sight more serious than he was used to. Mostly, people he knew had business disagreements, or whatever the likes of

Bernie Walters would call it, they went round each other's yard with a shotgun. They didn't have spies ringing them up and telling them who's been visiting the other guy.

'Yeah, that's right,' he said, 'I went round to see Billy on Saturday. And you know why I went round there? I went round to tell him I'm out of the life. He wants to go up against Kenny, that's his business. And that's the same thing I'm telling you. It's not what I'm into now.'

Tony started to get up from the table but Bernie waved him back down.

'I appreciate that, Tony, and I admire that. Just the qualities that make me think you'd be ideal for the job I was talking about. And I'm serious about that. Don't matter to me you've been inside. I've been in this business long as I have 'cause I like to think I have instincts about people, and you're all right, son, I can see that. And, let's face it, there aren't a lot of jobs around.' Here the words trailed off and Bernie looked Tony square in the eyes.

Tony stared back thinking, I should just get up now and keep walking. But he didn't. Bernie was right. What choice did he have?

'What do you want?' he said.

'Just the word, Tony, just a word. You go see your cousin Billy, and tell him you need a little earner, whatever, get back on side with him, and when he tells you what he's planning, you tip uncle Bernie the good word. And that's it.'

'Right,' said Tony. 'That's all, is it? Sell out my cousin to some bloke buys me a plate of spaghetti, tells me my cousin's a grass.' He shook his head.

'Tell you what,' said Bernie. 'Why don't you think it over, ask about a bit and then let me know? I'll be there till eight.

That's when the offer closes.' Bernie stood up, put a couple of twenties down on the table and started out of the restaurant. Tony was going to let him go, but then something occurred to him and he got up too and caught Bernie up as they emerged on to the street.

'Did you ever know a singer called April Angel?' he asked.

Bernie came to a dead halt. 'Jesus,' he said, 'I haven't heard that name in thirty years. April Angel. Christ. Tell you what, son, I've been working in clubs my whole bloody life and I never saw another girl like that. April Angel. So what made you ask that?'

'She's my mother,' said Tony.

It wasn't something you saw often, someone with an orange tan as fervent as Bernie Walters's go completely white, but that's what happened then. 'Oh my God,' he said after a moment. 'You're April's son.'

'What I said,' said Tony, wondering what the hell was going on.

Bernie stared at him, his colour gradually returning. 'Tell you what, son, whatever you decide, come back to my office later, round seven o'clock. You and me better have a chat.' And before Tony could say anything more, Bernie was off, moving fast through the shoppers.

Tony headed back towards Butetown, his head overloading. He hadn't gone far when he realised he needed a drink and a piss, so he stopped into the Custom House. He had a word with Wariq behind the bar, a game of pool with Bobby who beat him on the black which showed his concentration had gone, and then sat down by himself for a while, trying to figure out where the hell to go from here.

Way he saw it, he was trapped like a lab rat. Whatever he

did, he was screwed. No way he was going to grass up his cousin Billy on the one side. Family got to mean something, and Bernie's story about Billy could be true but was most likely just hot air. Other hand, though, God knows he could do with that job, if that wasn't bullshit as well. Only chance he had, far as he could see, to get Tyra back: get a decent job, show her he could do it. But he didn't turn Billy over – no fucking job. Life, he thought, total crock of shit. For a moment he even thought fondly of being inside. Least you didn't have crap choices like this to make.

He finished his drink and walked back out into the afternoon sun, absolutely no clearer as to what he should do. His feet led him automatically down Crichton Street and left into East Canal Wharf, taking the back way into Butetown. Distracted as he was, it took him a second or two to register the car coming up slowly behind him, and, before he could properly react, a side door had opened and a guy jumped out and pressed a blade against Tony's back.

The guy was a total amateur; Tony threw himself forward and down, away from the blade, causing the knife-man to lose his balance. As Tony fell, he twisted and kicked backwards, tripping the guy. Tony was on his feet in two seconds flat and his left foot stamped down on the knife-man's hand. Two more seconds, and the knife was in Tony's hand, the other hand holding on to the guy's throat.

Tony had never seen the guy he was holding on to before, but by now the driver had got out of the car and Tony knew him all right. Gary something or other, one of Billy's Ely boys. Gary kept his distance. He knew better than to come anywhere near Tony, any time he had a knife in his hand.

'Fuck's going on, Gary?' said Tony, ignoring the kid –

that's all he was, some stupid kid in a Calvin Klein jacket thought he was about ten times harder than he actually was.

'Nothing, Tone. Billy just wanted a word, that's all.'

'And that's what he thinks he needs to do, have a word with me? Send some YTS villain round to stick a penknife in my back. Fuck's sake.' Suddenly Tony brought his head down hard on the kid's nose. Blood started flowing at once and Tony pushed the kid away. 'Fuck off now,' he said, 'back to the playground.'

The kid did as he was told, walked off towards town, fast as he could go without looking like he was running.

'Come on then,' said Tony. 'Let's go and see Billy, he wants a word with me.'

Gary shrugged, said, 'That's what I told him, Tone. But Billy's a bit hyper, like, at the moment and that lad Kelvin's looking to impress him, and that's what you get, this kind of situation. A cock-up.'

Tony just shook his head and the rest of the drive up to Ely passed off in silence.

Billy must have been watching for the car, as the door opened as soon as Tony got out.

'Sorted out Kelvin then,' he said, apparently cheery as ever.

Tony stared at him but Billy carried on. 'Thought I'd give him a taste of playing the big leagues, like.'

'Fuck you, Billy.'

'Yeah, well, thought you might take it like that. Come on in.'

'No,' said Tony, 'you send Gary in, then you and me can get in the car and have a little drive back down town, drop me off there.'

Billy shrugged. 'Your call, Tony. What you think, I've got

an ambush waiting for you inside? Got Stacey there with a shotgun?'

'Wouldn't know, Billy, would I?' said Tony.

Billy shrugged again, motioned for Gary to get inside. Gary tossed him the car keys and the cousins got into the car.

'You grass me up, Billy?' said Tony once they'd turned into Cowbridge Road.

'That what he told you, this Bernie Walters fella?'

Tony nodded.

'Bollocks, Tony. Police screwed the case up fair and simple. You think they're going to make themselves look that stupid just to let me off, when they had me red-handed? Don't think so, Tone. Thanks for giving me Walters's name, though. Knew Kenny was hooked up with someone but I didn't know who. So what's he want, Tony? What's he talking to you about?'

'Nothing. Same old bullshit you're giving me. Kenny and him wants me, you wants me, every fucker wants me. How many times I got to tell you all I'm out of it?'

'Yeah?'

'Yeah?'

Billy shook his head. 'I'm surprised, Tony. You ain't seen Tyra yet?'

'Yeah, this morning.'

'Didn't she tell you 'bout Kenny?'

'Said she borrowed some money off him, yeah.'

'Tell you how she paid him back?'

There was a silence. Tony stared at Billy, then he said, 'Billy, you better be telling me something real. ' 'Cause you lie to me now, I'll cut your face off.'

Billy raised his hands from the steering wheel momentarily,

held them up pacifyingly. 'Tone, this is what I've heard. Can't swear I seen it myself, 'cause I haven't, but it's what I heard, right. You know how it goes, you borrow off Kenny. Two hundred, that's twenty a week; four hundred, that's forty. You miss one week, pay double next week. You miss two weeks, you're screwed. Yeah?'

Tony nodded.

'Yeah, well, Tyra don't have the money, do she? So what's she going to do to get it? Get a job. Sure, I bet she tried, but with the kids and all it's not easy. And she's a good-looking woman, Tone, always has been.'

'What're you saying, Billy?'

'What I'm saying, Tone, is that Kenny, your old mate, gave your woman so much grief 'bout this little two hundred pound, she ends up out hustling over Riverside.'

Tony had seen it coming but he still wasn't prepared. As Billy spoke, a white mist came down, blurring his vision. For a moment he thought he might start crying, but he bit his lip and rocked back and forward in his seat and kept the tears back, let the anger course through his veins instead.

'Who told you?'

'Don't matter who told me, Tone.'

'I asked you a fucking question. Who told you?'

Billy shrugged. 'What it's worth, Tone, it was a girl called Pauline, friend of Stacey's, works down there from time to time. Told Stacey she'd seen Tyra on the beat. Sorry, Tone.'

Tony didn't say a word. Just sat there in the passenger seat, staring blindly out at the shoppers on Clare Street, feeling like he was ready to explode with anger, but unable to decide where to go with it.

Kenny was looking favourite for it, if what Billy was telling him was true. Which was still a pretty big if. 'Cept it explained why Tyra was so angry with him. Christ. Thing he couldn't escape, though, was that, even if it was true, then maybe it wasn't Kenny's fault. Tyra certainly didn't think so. She wasn't blaming Kenny; you borrowed off Kenny, you knew what you were doing. She just hadn't had a choice. And why hadn't she had a choice? 'Cause of him, 'cause he'd been sitting in jail like a twat. And why had he been in jail? 'Cause he'd gone along with the idiot sitting next to him.

'So you going to come in with me, bra?' said Billy. 'Give Kenny a piece of what he deserves.' They were in Butetown now; Billy stopped the car across the way from Pearl's place. Tony just opened the door and was about to get out without saying anything, but, as he got up from his seat, Billy leaned over and said, 'Wednesday night, bra, that's when the boat comes in.'

Tony walked away from the car without a word, heading for Pearl's. But as he saw Billy pull a U-turn and head back over the Grangetown bridge, he switched direction and headed for Tyra's place. His place. He came round the back door. Most people did. Front door was for official visits.

He got as far as the yard gate and then he stopped. The kitchen light was on and he could see Tyra in there – making the kids' tea, he supposed. It was dark enough now, though, at six o'clock, that there was little chance she could see him standing out there. Which was lucky, as he suddenly realised he couldn't move. Couldn't step forward or back; he was just stuck there, rooted to the spot, contemplating what he'd done to the best person he knew. He wanted, he wanted with every fibre of his being to blame someone else. He had the knife – Christ, he had the knife gripped in his hand – and he knew if he saw Kenny right that moment he would probably go for him. But he couldn't sustain it, couldn't keep the blame anywhere except on his own head.

He might have stood there all night if he hadn't heard footsteps after a while and seen old Mrs Watkins from next door coming his way. Tony turned on his heel then and headed back towards Bute Street. Checking his watch, he saw it was half six; half an hour must have gone by as he stood staring through the window. It was time to pay another visit to Bernie Walters.

He hadn't seen it before, but this time it was the first thing he noticed in Bernie's office, the framed ten-by-eight glossy of April Angel. It was right there on the wall next to the picture of Bernie with one arm round George Mr Speaker Thomas, and the other round a fixer named Jack Brooks, sunny Jim Callaghan's right-hand man, ended up as Lord Splott or something. In fact, you looked closely, the room was plastered in pictures of Cardiff's movers and shakers over the last forty years. There was John Toshack handing Bernie a copy of his book, *Gosh, It's Tosh*, William Hague looking about twelve handing Bernie some kind of award, Ray Reardon handing him a snooker cue, too many opera singers and rugby players to count. And of course there was a picture of Shirley Bassey. How could there not be?

'I booked her at the beginning, you know,' said Bernie.

'Who? My mum?'

'No, well, I did book your mum, of course. But I was talking about Shirley. She had it right from the start, you know. Little girl from Butetown, knew she was ready to take on the world. 'Course she'd already been up to London, been in a couple of shows by the time I worked with her. I put her on at the Capitol. Packed. Could have sold it three times over, really got me started in the industry. You remember the Capitol, Tony?'

Tony nodded, 'course he remembered the Capitol. First big show he ever went to, Earth, Wind and Fire at the Capitol, seventy-five or -six. Went with Debbie, his first kid's mum. She was pregnant then. She was nineteen, he was only fifteen. Christ, weird when you thought about it now; the kid, Lorraine, she must be grown up by now. Hadn't seen her since she was six; Debbie buggered off to Swindon, married some RAF guy. He didn't blame her, never had.

'No, butt,' he said finally, 'I don't remember the Capitol or the bloody trolley buses or the sodding Kardomah, or the bloody Casablanca, come to that. I just came here 'cause you said you knew something about my mum, so let's have it.'

Bernie raised his hand. 'Take it easy, son,' he said. 'Have a drink.' He got up from behind his desk and walked over to a cocktail cabinet topped by a picture of the cricketer Tony Lewis, took out a half-empty bottle of flash-looking whisky and poured Tony a whacking great glass of the stuff.

'Right then,' he said, once he'd returned to his own drink. 'What d'you want to know about April, then? Or I suppose you think of her as Fatima, do you?'

'No,' said Tony, 'I think of her as Mum.'

'You know it was me came up with the name,' said Bernie, rattling on oblivious. 'April 'cause that's when her birthday was, Angel because that's the first thing I ever said to her. You sing like an angel, I said to her down the old Ocean Club, and she laughed and laughed at me but after that I just used to say "Hiya, angel" when I saw her and it kind of stuck. She was one of the best, you know, your mum. Back then there weren't a lot of girls could sing the American stuff; you know, the rhythm and blues. GIs used to come down to Butetown every weekend, brought their records – great stuff, you know, all those vocal groups, the Moonglows and the Five Satins and those dance records, Ivory Joe Hunter, Ray Brown. You could hear all that stuff down Butetown no one else ever heard of till the sixties. And all the singers down here had a go. Shirley even did a few, but it was always show tunes she liked. Lorne Lesley wasn't bad either, but your mum was the best. Took her up to London, must have been 1959, signed her up to Decca, you ever hear that record she made?'

Tony shook his head.

' "In the Still of the Night". You know that song?' Suddenly Bernie launched into a couple of bars. 'Anyway, she did it fabulous and then they stuck this horrible bloody orchestra on it and screwed the whole thing up. I was absolutely bloody tamping mad about it at the time. Funny thing was, your mum didn't seem to care that much. 'Course it wasn't long after that you came along and I, we . . .'

Bernie came to a pause and Tony could sense rapid calculation going on behind his eyes.

'Yeah, well,' he went on. 'One thing or another, I didn't see much of April after you were born. I was up in London most of the sixties. Fantastic time, the sixties, never be another like it. Anyway, your mum kept busy doing the club circuit down here, far as I know, and I didn't hear from her at all. Not for a long time.'

Bernie stood up, walked over to the drinks cabinet. All of a sudden, Tony noticed he'd started to sweat. 'Another drink?' Bernie said, pouring himself a tumblerful of pure Scotch. Tony shook his head.

'So you heard from her again?' prompted Tony after a while, as Bernie sat back behind his desk and went to work on the whisky.

'Oh yes. I heard from her once more.'

'When?'

'1970, I think it was, thereabouts anyway. I remember it was the week the Beatles split up. You like the Beatles, Tony? I never thought they were much, to be honest.'

'1970,' Tony cut in, trying to get the increasingly drunk Walters back on track, 'that's when she left us.'

'Yeah, son, I know that. Look, there isn't an easy way to tell you this. But here goes. That's why your mum called me up, she wanted to get out and she'd heard I'd been booking acts abroad. Cruises and resorts and stuff. So she asked me if I could get her something, anything really, she said, long as it was out of the country. I made a few calls and I got her a nice little cruise job, round the Med.'

'That's why she left us, to go on a cruise?'

'Hardly, son; no, that was the only thing going. What I heard was after that she went to Marbella, got a residency in one of the clubs there, in the yacht place they have down there, Puerto something or other. You ever been out there, Tony?'

'Get lost,' said Tony. 'Why did she go, then? Did she tell you that?'

Once again Bernie hesitated before talking, and poured another large one. 'Your dad,' he said then. 'He's dead now, right?'

Tony nodded, wondering why Bernie would have known that.

'Well, your dad was a jealous man. And, I mean, who could

blame him? He was married to a woman like April, beautiful and out there singing in the clubs with men hitting on her all the time, and your dad he was off at sea a lot of the time. Not surprising he was jealous. But round the time you were born, he started getting really bad. That was the real reason I stopped working with your mum, you want to know the truth, 'cause Everton, your dad, told her to get rid of me, he was going to be her manager. Which, between you and me, if you bear in mind that he didn't know a thing about the business, is why your mum spent the sixties playing the Trafalgar Club, Caerphilly when she should have been at the London Palladium.'

Suddenly Bernie came to a full stop, and when he started talking again it was like he was talking to himself. 'I loved her, you know,' he said. 'But it was different back then, the fifties, my family would have killed me.'

'You've lost me now, boss,' said Tony. 'What I want to know is, you've got any idea where she is now?'

For a while it was as if Bernie was too wrapped up in memory to have heard him but then he shook himself and said, 'No idea, son. But you never know, I might know a man who does. Give me a couple of days and I'll see what I can do. And how about you, son, you thought about what we talked about? You going to help Kenny out with your cousin?'

'Tomorrow,' said Tony, 'I'll talk to you tomorrow.' And, with that, he stood up. As he walked through the darkened outer office, he turned his head slightly to catch sight of Bernie Walters going over to the whisky bottle once more.

Heading back up towards Butetown, Tony felt overwhelmed by a sense of dread. It had started that morning with Tyra when she'd been giving him all that grief. Thinking about his dad. Memories coming back. His dad shouting. The way the house would be just before his dad was due back from sea. Frightened. Shit, he didn't want any of this. Not many things he knew in life, but he knew his dad had loved him. His dad had stayed with them, hadn't he? His dad hadn't gone off on no cruise ship, had he? But, shit. His mother crying.

Without conscious thought, his feet had taken him to Mandy's place. She widened her eyes when she saw him, then led him into the kitchen where she was preparing some pasta.

'Kids in bed?' he asked.

'Yeah,' she said. 'What's up with you? You look like you've seen a ghost.'

'Near enough,' he said, and, as she added more tagliatelle to the saucepan, cooked it up and served it out for the two of them, he told her about his meeting with Bernie Walters.

'Whoo,' said Mandy when he finished. 'You don't think he's your dad, do you?'

'What?' said Tony, completely blindsided.

'Bernie Walters. You don't think he could be your dad, do you? I mean, what he was saying about your dad being jealous around when you were born, and Bernie pissing off to London. You don't think —'

'Nah, Christ's sake, Mand, he's a white guy, isn't he?'

'Yeah, well,' said Mandy, shrugging and backing off.

Tony stayed silent for a moment. It was true he was light-skinned, but then so was his mum. He'd just assumed he took after her, but that could work both ways . . . Then he shook his head firmly. No way. 'Hell of a thing to say, Mand, you know that.'

She put her hands up. 'Yeah, sorry, Tone, I just got caught up in the story. Reading too many of them Catherine Cooksons, you know what I mean. Always turns out people's dads aren't who they're supposed to be.'

'Yeah, well,' he said. 'Anyway, it's the least of my problems, really, all that crap. Real question is what am I going to do about Kenny and Billy?' He shook his head. 'Shit, Mand, I swear it's doing my head in, stuff's being going on today. Billy told me Tyra been hustling while I was inside. Did you know that?'

Mandy frowned. 'First I've heard of it, Tone. But' – and her voice was harder now – 'that's the kind of thing happens, your man goes away. Tone, you've got to keep out of this shit with Kenny and Billy. Don't matter who done what to who, you get involved it's going to be you who gets screwed again. Best thing you can do for Tyra and the kids, keep out of it.'

Tony stood up. 'Yeah, you're right,' he said. 'I better get back to Pearl's. I've got the kids tomorrow after school, you want to meet up?'

'Maybe. Call me. And remember what I said. Stay out of it.'

Tony just managed to keep his eyes open long enough to watch *News at Ten* with Pearl before he crashed into bed. The night seemed to go on for ever. Dream after dream assailed him. In one he was in a nightclub. Tyra and the children were there somewhere, he knew it, so he went upstairs. There was an empty dance floor there and he walked to the edge to see if he could find them. Suddenly he realised there was no floor in this part of the room, just a fragile latticework of thin metal strips that didn't look like they'd support the weight of a cat.

He jumped on to the window sill only to find there was no glass and he was swaying out over the lights of the city. The only way to safety was across the metal latticework. Nothing for it: he had to walk across it, had to push forward off each strand as it collapsed beneath him. And somehow he did it, made it back to the empty dance floor. When he woke up from this one, his heart was going like a steam hammer.

After that he stayed awake for hours trying to make some sense of that overload of information he'd been receiving. When he came out of prison, he'd at least believed he knew who his family were. Now his wife – and he couldn't blame her – wanted shot of him, and some damn golf-club guy seemed to know more about his own parents than he did.

One way or another, then, Tony didn't feel much like getting up come morning. Instead he just lay in bed and smoked and tried to construct some kind of plan. Around lunchtime it came to him.

First thing he did was bell Mikey and arrange to see him round the Ship. Mikey was half an hour late, as per usual, but he looked a lot more relaxed this time. Which left him completely unprepared for Tony's first words.

'I hear you've been messing round with my woman while I was inside.'

Tony was staring straight at Mikey as he said it, and he knew at once from the horror on Mikey's face that it was true. Funny thing was, he wasn't that bothered. It was like he'd already accepted that Tyra was gone from him, so what she did was her own business. He wasn't going to let Mikey know that, though. Mikey was going to suffer.

Mikey bullshitted and burbled away. 'Wasn't like you think, Tone. Only one time, bra. I'd . . . I'd helped her out, like, and she was grateful and lonely, you know, Tone. And, Christ, you knows what I'm like. But it's you she cares about, Tone, you know what I mean.'

Tony just sat there, giving Mikey the stare, letting him imagine the beating he was going to get. Then he leaned forward and said, 'Mikey. Shut up.'

Mikey shut up.

'You know what you done, I should fuck you up.'

Mikey nodded, his eyes moving swiftly round the room looking for potential allies.

'But I got a better idea. You're going to give me a bit of help, like.'

Mikey nodded again, his eyes narrowing this time. Then Tony leaned in close to him and told him what he wanted. As he finished, Mikey's head started to shake but then he saw the look Tony was giving him and abandoned the movement. Instead he said, 'What's in it for me, bra?'

'Ten per cent, off the top, and your dick gets to stay attached to the rest of your body.'

Mikey shook his head once again. 'Better pray to fuck this works, Tone, or none of us are going to be putting it round much any more.' Then, Mikey being Mikey, he brightened. 'Anyway, you been getting any since you been out? Tyra have you back yet?'

Tony stood up. 'Leave it,' he said, 'just leave it. And be there tomorrow, all right?'

Tony just had time to get back to the house and warm up some stew Pearl had left on the stove when Tyra brought the kids round. Tyra herself was gone the second the words 'Bring them back by seven' were out of her mouth, but seeing the kids, Jermaine and Latasha, was enough to take the bitterness out of the situation. Latasha, who was five, just threw herself at Tony, leaped up into his arms, while seven-year-old Jermaine stood there trying to look cool but with a huge grin across his face, so Tony scooped him up too.

For the next ten minutes or so they sat there, wrestling on Auntie Pearl's sofa, just happy to be together. But then, just as suddenly, the kids' mood seemed to change, like they'd seen enough of Dad now and it was time to go home. Tony realised he'd better do something with them. He looked out the window and properly registered for the first time that it was a beautiful day out there. A plan came to him. A quick phone call, and it was put into action.

He herded the kids out of the house and down the road, cutting through Mount Stuart Square and along to Mandy's place. Mandy had her two kids ready to go and the six of them squeezed into Mandy's car, an ageing Sierra, coming round the clock for the second time.

Fifteen minutes later, they were in Roath Park, an Edwardian oasis in the suburban north-east of the city.

'Any of you kids ever been in a boat before?' Tony asked.

The kids all shook their heads and Tony felt a swell of enthusiasm for life as he led the way alongside the boating lake to the boathouse itself. A little while later, and the whole troupe were waterborne and all laughing at Tony as he turned the boat in a complete circle and crashed back into the dock, trying to remember how to row. Still, a bit of perseverance and he got the hang of it, and then, out in the middle of the lake, the spring sun as hot as he could remember it in April, his kids beside him and a woman he loved opposite. Jesus, he thought to himself, woman he loved, where did that come from? It was Mandy opposite him. Like a sister to him; Christ, she was still a young girl. He pulled himself up again, thought about it for a moment. If he was thirty-six, that made Mandy thirty-one. Christ, but the years creep up on you. 'Specially if you make a habit of spending them in prison.

They circled round the little wooded island in the middle of the lake and the kids started clamouring to get off and explore. Tony looked at Mandy, who smiled and shrugged back at him, so he nosed the row boat in as close as he could and the kids took off their shoes and socks, rolled up their tracksuit bottoms and waded on to the island. Mandy stood up and moved over to sit next to Tony. Tony was about to say something fatuous, like nice day for it, but before the words were out of his mouth Mandy said shhh, and then her lips were on his and then her tongue snaking between them, and then suddenly both their mouths opened and they were doing their best to devour each other.

'Christ,' said Tony, as they came up for air. It was all he could say, caught up as he was in a rush of excitement and alarm. The excitement of the first kiss coupled with a sense of horror that she was virtually his sister, and worse yet the realisation that that only made it more exciting. Thank God for the virtually, really.

He leaned back a little and twisted his head round to look at Mandy and was relieved to see that she was grinning like the cat with the cream. 'Shit, Tone,' she said, 'if you knew how long I'd wanted to do that.'

And then the kids were back, almost tipping the boat over as they clambered back on.

'So who fancies an icecream then?' said Tony, and four little voices assented and Tony put his back into rowing them back to the boathouse. Cones of Thayers chocolate were duly dispensed all round and the return home passed in a blur. The only thing to stick in Tony's mind being Mandy's lips close to his ear saying 'Come round later' as she dropped him and the kids off back at Pearl's.

Tony walked the kids round to Tyra's, hoping to hell they hadn't seen him kissing Mandy, last thing he wanted Tyra to know. Or maybe it wasn't, maybe he didn't care. Shit, what was happening to his life? You spent all those days in prison where no fucking thing happened, the nearest thing to excitement when he won the table-tennis tournament on his block, and now the world seemed to be rushing at him, keeping him permanently off balance.

Tyra didn't ask him in or anything but she gave him a little bit of a smile, which was something, and asked if he'd like to see them again on Friday and he said yes. And it was only as he turned and left, after giving the kids one last hug, that he realised it was a lie. No way he was going to be seeing his kids on Friday if what he was planning went off right. Or went off wrong, come to that. Likelihood was he wouldn't be seeing anyone on Friday, it went off wrong.

Walking back to Pearl's, he was too preoccupied to register at first that Pearl was talking to someone. Col was sitting there in the living-room chatting away with the old lady about the latest things going on with the bay development. A lot of the old-timers couldn't see anything good about the way things were going, spent their whole time reminiscing about the old bay. Pearl, however, was a more realistic soul and had little nostalgia for living in a slum, and she was excited by all the new stuff springing up now. So she and Col were talking away, apparently oblivious, when Tony walked in.

It was obvious, though, that there was only one reason for Col to be there, and so it proved.

'Let's go for a drink,' said Col, after a couple more minutes' chat with the old lady. 'Kenny's over the Ship.'

Tony shrugged, said, 'Why not?' and headed out into the night with Col, wondering what the hell he was walking into.

Tony needn't have worried; he played it perfectly. Yes, he told Kenny, he'd met Bernie. Yes, he'd heard about Billy. No, he couldn't believe what the bastard had done to him. Yes, Billy had approached him. Yes, Billy was planning something tomorrow night. Yes, he, Tony, would be happy to play along with Billy and then sell him out to Kenny when the time came.

Kenny was happy, Kenny was thrilled. Kenny let Tony in on the plans. The drugs were indeed coming in on the Trinidad boat tomorrow night. The deal was going to go down in the Casablanca at nine. All Tony had to do was tell Billy the wrong time. Tell him to be there at eight o'clock, then Kenny and his guys could ambush the ambushers. Simple.

Couple more drinks, then, to seal the deal, and Kenny headed over to Caesar's. Col and Tony sat over their drinks a little while longer.

'How's it with Tyra?' Col asked.

Tony shook his head. 'Seriously pissed off with me, bra.' There was more he wanted to say but realised he couldn't. He wanted to know if Col had known about Kenny and Tyra's loan, but he couldn't risk sounding critical of Kenny. The other thing he felt like asking was about Col's baby mother, Maria. She was a hustler. He wondered now how Col had handled that. But it wasn't, to be honest, the kind of thing guys like him talked about. He was starting to wonder a little about that. Wondering why he'd spent so much of his life learning to be so damn hard. Still, that would have to wait; next couple of days he was going to have to be every bit as hard as they come if he wanted to walk out the other side. So he changed the subject, laughed and joked a little, then told Col he had to go.

Col laughed and said, 'You got a woman waiting,' and Tony laughed too and said, 'Yeah, man,' and clashed fists with Col and walked back into the night, letting the cool air sober him up as he headed round to Mandy's place.

Later he would wonder if it was just the tension of his whole situation, the total chaos that was engulfing his life, that made what happened next feel so powerful. There was no question about what was going down from the moment he opened the door. It was dark and quiet in the house, the kids were in bed asleep, Mandy was in a nightdress and her bedroom was lit by candles. What happened next was just the usual stuff that happens when a man and a woman get together in a bedroom in the candlelight, but for both of them it was the same but different, the same but better, the same but so good that it left both of them close to tears afterwards.

Somewhere towards morning, Tony asked Mandy a question.

'What'd you say to going to Spain for a while, you and me and the kids?'

'Spain,' she said sleepily. 'What's in Spain?'

'My mum, maybe.'

'Oh,' she said, 'yeah, sounds nice,' and wrapped her arm round him.

'Seriously,' he said. 'Let's go to Spain.'

'Mmmm.'

'Tomorrow.'

'What?' said Mandy. 'Better wait till the holidays,' a faint note of anxiety coming into her voice. Tony decided to leave it, turned round again to face her and stopped talking, let his finger trace a line from her collarbone to her nipple.

In the morning Tony dozed fitfully while Mandy got the kids ready for school and nursery. By the time she came back, though, he was up and dressed and they had a little breakfast together before Mandy had to be in work, over the pub.

Tony walked out with her and kissed her long and hard goodbye, but was by then actually relieved to be on his own. He had a lot to think about, he was going to make it through to the end of the day.

First he made a phone call to a London number, one he'd acquired in prison. Then, satisfied with the ensuing conversation, he took the bus out to Ely, walked round to Billy's place. He did exactly what Kenny had told him to do. Told Billy he was prepared to help him ambush Kenny. Billy smiled big. Then Tony told Billy what he wanted. A quarter share off the top, whatever they got away with.

Billy said no problem, cuz, no problem. So what's the plan? Simple, Tony told him, the deal goes down in the Casa. Be round the back at eight o'clock. I'll open the back door for you. Come in fast and hard and it's all yours.

Billy wanted Tony to hang around, smoke a little draw – or something a little stronger if you're up for it, bra, get you up big time.

Tony shook his head, said he'd better get back, didn't want Kenny getting suspicious. So Billy had Gary drive Tony back into town, dropped him off by the ice rink, just over from the Bute Street bridge. But Tony didn't head on into Butetown, like he told Gary he was going to do. Instead he waited till Gary had pulled a Uey across the six lanes of traffic and headed back up to Ely, then he walked round to the bus station. There he went into the café, got a coffee and sat down at a window table on the side looking out at Wood Street. A half hour later, almost exactly on three o'clock, he saw a black Saab 900 with London plates pull up on the double yellow lines and, when the window wound down to reveal a familiar face, Tony walked out of the café and got into the car.

At six o'clock Tony met up with Col, Kenny and one of Kenny's cousins, a hard boy named Darrell, in the Ship.

'All set, boss,' said Tony.

Kenny didn't say anything, just raised his giant fist and clashed it against Tony's.

'Billy'll be coming round the back around eight,' Tony went on.

'Any idea how many?'

Tony shook his head. 'Gary, I expect. Maybe this kid called Kelvin. Dunno who else, could be any of the Ely boys. Don't reckon more than a carful, though, if they're going to try to sneak up quiet, like.'

'Don't matter, we'll be ready for them. Won't forget this, bra.'

Col stood up then. 'Going up town,' he announced. 'Little bit of business. You fancy coming along, bra?' he said to Tony.

Before Tony could answer, Kenny cut in. 'You'll be staying here, see how things work out, won't you, Tone.'

He didn't put any menace in it. That was the thing with

Kenny: he didn't have to come on like a thug all the time; you just had to look at him to know you didn't want to cross him, and evidently what Kenny wanted was to keep Tony where he could see him. Suited Tony too, but he let a glimmer of irritation cross his face, like he couldn't believe Kenny didn't trust him.

'You're not staying around yourself then?' he said to Col.

'Nah, too old for this business, man. Stick to mi retail activities, you know what I'm saying.' And, with that, he was off.

Tony stayed in the pub for another half hour, then Kenny led the way over to the Casa. They went in through the front door, and Kenny locked it behind them before ushering them over to a table by the bar. Over the next half hour four more of Kenny's guys showed up. Younger faces that Tony knew, but wouldn't have thought ready for this kind of serious business. But that's what a year out of circulation could do. Made you lose your sense of who's who. Some boys grew up quick in the bad-man business. They all said hello to Tony and he was pleased to see they gave him a little bit of respect, though there was none of the fear there he used to get off guys who'd seen him in action.

But then two of the guys at least had shooters, and Tony had never been comfortable around shooters. Partly for the obvious reason. Shooters killed people, even if you weren't trying to. Not like a knife, where you could use a bit of judgement. And where you needed a bit of skill and a bit of courage. Going up against someone with a knife was an art. Any twelve-year-old could pull a trigger. Other thing was if you got shooters involved, they threw away the key, turned a one-year sentence into five. He couldn't stop himself from letting out a sigh. Christ, he hoped he'd get through this one. Cops showed up, he didn't know what he'd do. Still, one thing about working with Kenny, chances were the cops were squared away.

Between seven and eight the tension level in the room mounted steadily. The chit-chat had died out almost completely when, all of a sudden, Kenny said to Tony, 'Got a message for you, bra, from Bernie.'

'Oh yeah.'

'Yeah, it's about your mum. Bernie reckons he knows where she is.'

'Where?'

'Somewhere in Spain, bra. Porto something, I think, fucked if I can remember. But Bernie got the details. Christ, I thought your mum was dead.'

'No,' said Tony. 'Looks like she's alive.'

The room relapsed into silence after that till around quarter to. Then everyone took up their positions. Kenny and Tony sat round a table under the only light that was turned on in the whole place. They had a couple of bags out on the table. The bags were empty but anyone bursting in the back door would assume that this is where the deal was going down. With a bit of luck they wouldn't notice the four guys waiting in the shadows. The worry Tony had was that Billy's boys would just steam in shooting and that would be the end of him and Kenny. But he didn't really believe it. That wasn't the way things happened down here.

They all heard the car arrive round the back of the Casa. They all heard the doors open and then somebody curse as he tripped over some of the crap lying around in the back yard. They didn't so much charge through the back door as stumble

into it. There were four of them: Billy and Gary plus two
others Tony didn't know. The kid Kelvin wasn't there. Tony
hoped he'd realised he wasn't cut out for the life, but
suspected he'd probably just shot himself in the foot when
they were tooling up.

In fact Billy looked to be the only one who was armed. He
was swinging an evil-looking sawn-off and, to give him his
due, he at least made a go at carrying the thing off proper.
Second he saw Kenny sat at the table with someone, he swung
the shotgun up and told them not to move. As he advanced,
though, and saw it was Tony there, he couldn't resist giving
his cousin a wink and saying, 'Nice one, bra.' And as he did so
his posture relaxed slightly and he never even noticed Kenny's
boy Darrell come up behind him till it was far too late. All he
could do was half turn before Darrell's baseball bat caught him
across the neck and shoulders.

Billy went down hard, the way blokes who've been hit
with baseball bats tend to go, and within seconds the rest of
Billy's gang all found themselves looking down gun barrels,
courtesy of the young guys, all of whom, Tony had to say,
looked impressively calm.

That was it. About two minutes start to finish and Billy's
master plan was fucked. Tony wasn't surprised: it wasn't like
the raid on the bookie's had been a clockwork success either.
Face it: cousin Billy was, like 99 per cent of all known villains,
completely crap.

Tony stood up and walked over to where Billy was lying.
For a second he was worried that Billy was lying too still,
thought maybe the baseball bat had caught him on the temple
or something. But then Billy writhed a little and Tony stepped
back and just watched as Kenny organised the tying up of

Billy and his three guys, then packed them off into the storeroom with Darrell to watch over them, carrying Billy's own shotgun.

'Sort you cunts out later,' said Kenny.

Then it was back to the waiting. This time Tony found it almost unbearable. The others were more relaxed, figuring they'd done the hard bit, but, by the time the drug guys from the ship turned up, Tony felt like he was about to explode.

There were two of them. The one you'd remember was a white guy, who had to be one of the three or four biggest people Tony had ever seen in his life. Not many people made Kenny look small but this feller did. The other guy was a wiry type who was completely unreadable. Could have been any age from thirty to fifty and could have come from any nation on earth. Neither of them looked too worried, despite the fact that the big guy was carrying three kilos of coke. Still, way Tony saw it, they must have done the risky stuff already, getting the gear off the boat. It wasn't likely Kenny was going to try and rip them off, not if he wanted to do any more business. No sense in cutting off your own supply.

In fact they were in and out of the Casa in fifteen minutes flat. Quick hellos between Kenny and the wiry guy, Kenny had a look at the merchandise, a little taste from a couple of bags, pronounced it good and produced a briefcase full of fifties, counted out thirty grand. A little bit more chat then, a quiet word between Kenny and the guy. Setting up the next deal, Tony supposed, and they were off. The big guy never said a word the whole time.

Things went perfectly after that, far as Tony was concerned. First thing was – he'd hoped for it, but hardly believed it would happen – Kenny and the boys decided to have a little tasting session. Tony, hanging back, looking like he was waiting his turn, was the only one who heard the faint sound of a car door opening somewhere out the back.

Tony exhaled with relief. That meant Mikey had done his stuff. Seconds later they were in there, the three London guys. And the lead guy, Trey, the one Tony had roomed with down Dartmoor, was carrying an automatic pistol. Tony thought it might have been a Glock but he wasn't sure. He didn't know shit about guns.

Anyway, it did the business. Kenny and his boys were caught completely off guard, noses in the trough. Trey kept his gun on Kenny. The second guy, a tall fella with a shaven head, grabbed Tony by the throat and held a gun to his temple. The third guy, a cheerful-looking bloke with a beard, opened up a holdall and swiftly scooped the money and drugs inside. Kenny half moved forward and Tony thought for a moment that he was so angry he might charge the gun. But he didn't; instead he slunk back down in his seat when Trey started shouting.

'Move another inch, I'll fucking kill you. We're going out now and, if any of you move a muscle, your mate here' – he pointed at Tony – 'he's dead. We're taking him with us. So don't none of yow move.' At the end there Trey even remembered to put on his best Brummie accent, the way Tony had told him to.

And, with that, the three guys moved backwards towards the door. One with the loot. One with the gun trained on Kenny and the boys. The other pushing Tony in front of him, gun to the back of Tony's head.

It was going perfectly. They were almost at the door. And then a voice came out of the shadows.

'Stop it right there.'

It was Darrell. Fuck. Tony had forgotten that Darrell had been in the storeroom guarding Billy and the boys.

It was a stand-off. Darrell came out of the shadows with the shotgun. Trey kept his gun on Kenny. Tony tensed up again. There seemed to be only two ways this was likely to go. Either they all stood there together for ever, or everyone was going to start firing and it was going to be a sodding blood-bath.

And then a miracle happened. Darrell's head was suddenly whipped back and a choking noise came from his throat. It was Billy. He'd come round. And now he had a piece of rope pulled tight round Darrell's neck. Then he chopped hard down on Darrell's arm and the shotgun fell to the floor.

The London guys didn't hesitate; the three of them and Tony were out of the back door in seconds. They all piled into the Saab and the driver had them moving out of there just as the first shot sounded from inside the Casa, Kenny and Billy going head to head.

'Fucking hell, bra, that sounded a bit close,' said the driver, as he screeched the Saab into a right turn past the police station and into Dumballs Road. Tony realised with mild surprise that it was Mikey, a baseball cap pulled low over his face, doing the driving. He'd rather thought that Mikey would have legged it once he'd done what Tony asked him to, shown the London guys where and when to hit the Casa. He'd probably hung around to make sure he got his share. Tony said nothing, just shook his head, waiting for his heartbeat to return to an acceptable level.

A couple of minutes later they were pulled up next to Mikey's old Datsun, round the back of a warehouse, right down the far end of Dumballs Road. The split was simple. Trey and the London guys took the coke and ten grand of the cash. Tony took the other twenty grand. Mikey got two grand from Tony's end and a baggie full of coke. Then the London guys were gone, heading straight out to the M4, and Tony and Mikey got into the Datsun.

'What the hell happened inside?' asked Mikey.

Tony ran through the edited highlights and Mikey whistled, said, 'He always did have a hard head, Billy.'

'Yeah, well,' said Tony. 'Be lucky to have a head at all by now, I should reckon.'

Mikey shrugged. 'Nah, once they realise the money and the drugs are gone, they'll probably calm down. Be too busy trying to chase after your mates there. Nice boys too, by the way. Now it's time I got home, put me feet up by the TV before Kenny gets the idea I might know something. And how about you, what you going to do? You think Kenny bought the hostage thing?'

'God knows. Don't worry 'bout me, Mikey. Tell you what, just drop me off by the Monument. And, listen, one thing you can do for me.'

'Yeah?' Mikey's tone was instantly guarded.

'Yeah.' Tony took an envelope out of his inside pocket and stuffed five grand or so into it. 'Next day or two take this round Tyra's, tell her I won it on the horses.' He stared at Mikey. 'And don't start thinking of ripping it off. I don't hear from Tyra she got it, you're dead.'

Mikey nodded, no problem, and, as the car pulled up to the lights, corner of Penarth Road and St Mary Street, Tony jumped out.

'Hey.' Mikey was leaning over, winding down the window. He raised his fist and Tony bent down and clashed fists. 'Take care, man,' said Mikey.

Tony scanned the road carefully for any sign of big Kenny's Land Rover and then sprinted across, and into Bernie's building.

Bernie was there in his office, glass of whisky next to his right hand.

'Tony,' he said, 'the very man.' Then he said it again. 'Tony, the very man.'

The state he was in, Tony wondered if he'd been sitting there drinking non-stop since the last time he'd seen him.

'My mum,' he said, 'Kenny says you know where my mum is.'

'No rush, son,' said Bernie, 'have a drink,' and he waved Tony towards a seat. In doing so, though, he must have caught a glimpse of the wildness in Tony's eyes, because then he said, 'Shit, where is it?' and started scrabbling around on his desk, evidently looking for a piece of paper. Eventually he came up with it. An envelope with an address jotted down on it. Tony leant over and took it from Bernie's hand.

'Sure you won't stay for a drink?'

'No thanks,' said Tony, looking down at the address which was indeed in Spain, a place called Sitges. 'Got a plane to catch.' And he turned to go.

'Wait,' said Bernie, suddenly sharper. 'You're going to see her?'

Tony nodded.

'Listen, then. You better know what happened. In fact, you coming in here like this, it's like a recur, a recurring, shit, I can't think of the word . . . Anyway, it's the same thing. I was sitting in this same office – what, getting on for thirty years ago – and she came in . . .'

'You told me she phoned you.'

'No, she came in. Listen. She came in and she looked like a ghost, she was so pale. She'd come straight from the hospital, she told me. He'd stabbed her.'

'Who had?'

'Your dad, of course. With a knife. Had a bit of a reputation, you know, Everton. With a knife.'

Bernie paused and Tony just stood there with his eyes squeezed tight shut wishing it would all go away. Then Bernie started talking again.

'That's why she went, Tony. She was in fear of her life. I told her to get a lawyer, but she just laughed, told me I didn't know him, didn't know what I was talking about. Then I said to her what about the kid and she said, quite calmly, like she'd been thinking about it, she said the kid will be fine. He loves Tony now.'

Bernie paused again and Tony was trembling all over. He was going to ask Bernie what he meant by that 'now'. Had his dad not loved him before? Was his dad even his dad? But before he could get a question out, he heard a noise from downstairs. Tony had pulled the downstairs door closed behind him, but there was a furious banging going on. Kenny. It had to be Kenny. He looked at Bernie and Bernie pointed a finger upwards and Tony said thanks and rushed up the stairs just as Bernie walked down them shouting, 'Calm down, who the hell's there?'

As Tony climbed the stairs, the successive storeys got shabbier and shabbier. The floor above Bernie's was just barely functional; a photocopied piece of paper stuck to a door proclaimed the existence of Raju Secretarial Services. The next floor, though, had clearly been unoccupied for years and he began to be aware of a strange noise – not coming from below, where he could hear a raised voice that sounded like Kenny, but from above.

He slowed down now, both trying to be quiet and because there was no light at all on this level. He gingerly felt his way up the stairs once more. Suddenly something brushed against his face and it was all he could do not to scream. Then another thing brushed his face, and another. Birds. There were birds flapping all around him.

As the staircase turned one last corner, there began to be a little more light. He could see the sky through the gaping holes in the roof above the next floor and there were birds absolutely everywhere, hundreds of them all flapping around in the confined space. The noise was incredible now and the smell of birdshit overpowering. He was looking frantically around for a way to climb up and out when he saw a side door. To get to it he fought his way through a phalanx of angrily flapping pigeons, but it was worth it when he opened the door and found himself on a roof terrace. He walked out and assessed his options.

There was a building on either side of him, but neither looked promising. The one to the right was easily accessible but it was the end of the line, the last building in the street. Still, Tony resolved to give it a try. He pulled himself up the six feet on to the next-door roof and wandered around looking for a fire escape or a way down inside. All he found was a firmly closed skylight and then a fire escape which went right down the front of the building. If Kenny was indeed in with Bernie, and he came back out on the street while Tony was climbing down, he'd be a sitting duck. He shook his head and jumped back down on the roof terrace he'd originally emerged on to. He'd have to try the other way.

One problem: there was a narrow alley, one he couldn't remember ever noticing at ground level, running between the two buildings. It was no more than six feet across and the other building was slightly lower down. So it was a simple enough jump. Except it would be difficult to build up much momentum, and, to be honest, heights were never Tony's thing. And, if he missed it, he died.

But then there was a sudden terrible sound of fluttering from the floor below and Tony figured someone was coming up the stairs. So he shut his mind down and went for it. And made it. Hurt his knee and scraped a load of skin off his right hand, but he made it. And, glory be, he was able to scuttle quickly along four more roofs in succession without having to climb or jump.

Then his progress came to a stop. He was three-quarters of the way along the block, and there were more rooftops ahead of him, but in between there was a valley. He looked down to see what was in the valley. Of course. It was the Wyndham Arcade, one of the many Edwardian shopping arcades that criss-crossed the city centre. Its glass-topped roof was a good storey lower than the buildings on either side of it. For a moment Tony thought he'd reached the end of his luck, then he noticed a little metal ladder going down the side of his building towards the glass roof. He climbed down and, just at the level of the glass roof, discovered a little walkway, running alongside it. He followed it to the northern end of the arcade where the walkway dead-ended in a door. Locked.

No problem. Tony gave the door the hearty shove of a

desperate man and it flew open. Down two flights of stairs and through an unmarked door, and he found himself in between the kitchen and toilets of the very same Italian restaurant he'd been in with Bernie just a day or two before.

Thanking God with all his heart, and looking around very carefully for Kenny's Land Rover, Tony crabbed his way past the Marriott and over into East Canal Wharf, kept to the shadows and in ten minutes found himself at Mandy's back door.

Mandy took one look at Tony and had him in and the door shut behind him before any of the neighbours could have blinked. She'd seen that kind of wild expression on too many men at her kitchen door not to recognise it for what it was. The face of someone hoping to hell they'd got away with something. And it was always followed by more visits — the police, more villains — it made little difference.

'What've you done?' she asked as Tony slumped down at her kitchen table.

He didn't say anything, just held out his arms to her, and, like a fool, like a lover, she succumbed, went to him, let him hold her. And was unutterably distressed to hear, for the first time in her life, the sound of Tony Pinto crying.

They stayed there for a while, her stroking his wiry hair while he sobbed into her breast. And then, just as suddenly as he'd started crying, he stopped. Held her a little way away from him so he could see her face and said, 'Come to Spain with me, Mand. I've got to see my mum.'

'What?' she said, joking. 'Tonight?'

'Yeah,' he said. 'Tonight.'

'You're crazy, man, what about the kids? You remember I have kids?'

'Bring 'em too.'

'Yeah, right,' she said. 'What about school? What about money?'

'Christ, Mand, they're only babies – won't matter if they miss school a few weeks. And I've got money, Mand. Don't worry about that.'

'What?' she said. 'What are you telling me not to worry about? Where'd you get the money, Tone?'

'Don't matter,' said Tony. 'Some people owed me and I collected, that's all. But we got to go now. Pack up the stuff and the kids, let's get out to the airport. There's a plane tonight. Midnight. Straight to Barcelona, Mand.'

Mandy just looked at him, not quite believing what was going on. And then suddenly she was swept up in it. Why the hell not? Wasn't this what she'd spent her life daydreaming about, getting out of this shithole? She'd got the passports and everything a few months back. When she'd told Linz she was going to take the kids out to see her dad in the States. Crazy cow she was, she almost believed it herself by now. Believed her dad was some millionaire in Florida or Hollywood or one of them places, not stuck up in Aberdeen where he'd gone to work on the rigs twenty years ago and never come back.

So she did it. She threw her stuff and the kids' stuff in a couple of bags. Woke the kids up and dressed them and loaded them in the back of the car. And half an hour later they were at Cardiff Airport, out past Barry.

It was standing in the ticket line, with her kids asking what was going on, that she came to her senses. Suddenly stood back from herself for a moment and saw what she was doing. Taking her children on a plane with a man who had – she just knew it – ripped off some money. She'd sworn she'd never do it again, never let her life be dominated by some man who would expose her to those dangers. She'd dumped Neville and she'd dumped fucking Jimmy Fairfax just to get out of that world, and now this . . .

Thing was, Tony was sweeter than the pair of them and what hurt was she was sure he could do better. And for another moment she let herself dream that maybe this was it, this was the start of Tony's new life and hers. Then she shook her head. Maybe if it had just been her, but not her kids too.

'Tony,' she said, 'I'm not going.'

The hurt on his face was painful to see.

'Mandy,' he said, 'you can't.' And he faltered. 'Mand,' he said, and she was sure he'd never in his hard life said his next words before; never in earnest, at least. 'I love you, Mand.'

'I know,' she said, but suddenly she was strong. She pulled him to her, kissed him hard and long, gave it everything she had. And then she said, 'Phone me, Tone. Phone me or write me from Spain. You get a life sorted out, out there – a legal life – you call me and I'll come. 'Cause you're not coming back, are you, Tone?'

'No,' he said, 'I'm not coming back.'

'Then send for me, Tony,' she said, and turned and led her children out of the airport and back to the car. The last thing Tony heard: the older kid Brittany asking, 'Where's he going, Mum? Where's that man going?'

About the Author

John Williams is a contributing editor at *GQ* and also a regular reviewer on various subjects: crime for the *Mail on Sunday*, fiction for the *Independent* and travel writer for the *Sunday Times*. He was born and lives in Cardiff although he has also lived in Paris and London where he worked in the music industry in various bands, before turning to writing as a career.